Darkman Fought the Rage That Tried to Block His Reason.

He turned and was able to get a hand on the knob and work the door open with a foot. He paused, beginning to breathe heavily.

The little girl in his arms lay motionless, but looking into her face he saw her eyelids flutter. He started out into the hall and nearly collided with a large man, who was hurrying down the hall.

The fat man swung up a shotgun in a swift motion and rested his finger on the trigger.

"What are you doing with her?" the man growled as he pumped a round into the chamber. "Who gave you permission to come up here?"

Darkman stared at him while his mind went absolutely blank, save for a large, seething area that was colored a bright and livid red, the red of his hate, the red of his rage that was slipping quickly, inexorably out of control.

Books in the DARKMAN™ Series

Published by POCKET BOOKS

For orders other than by individual consumers, Pocket Books grants a discount on the purchase of **10 or more** copies of single titles for special markets or premium use. For further details, please write to the Vice-President of Special Markets, Pocket Books, 1230 Avenue of the Americas, New York, NY 10020.

For information on how individual consumers can place orders, please write to Mail Order Department, Paramount Publishing, 200 Old Tappan Road, Old Tappan, NJ 07675.

DARKMAN #3™

THE GODS OF HELL

A NOVEL BY RANDALL BOYLL
BASED ON CHARACTERS CREATED BY CHUCK PFARRER AND SAM RAIMI &
IVAN RAIMI AND DANIEL GOLDIN & JOSHUA GOLDIN

POCKET BOOKS
New York   London   Toronto   Sydney   Tokyo   Singapore

This book is a work of fiction. Names, characters, places and incidents are products of the author's imagination or are used fictitiously. Any resemblance to actual events or locales or persons, living or dead, is entirely coincidental.

An *Original* Publication of POCKET BOOKS

POCKET BOOKS, a division of Simon & Schuster Inc.
1230 Avenue of the Americas, New York, NY 10020

Copyright © 1994 by MCA Publishing Rights,
a Division of MCA, Inc.

ISBN: 0-671-79435-3

First Pocket Books printing September 1994

10 9 8 7 6 5 4 3 2 1

POCKET and colophon are registered trademarks of Simon & Schuster Inc.

Printed in the U.S.A.

CHAPTER

1

The Tragedy

It was almost nine o'clock and Shawna Hastings had just brushed her teeth. She dropped by the living room to kiss her mother and father good night and then paused at the door of her bratty little sister's room long enough to give Tina a sneer and a toss of her head. Smiling, she aimed herself toward her own bedroom, glad that she was thirteen now and far past the brat stage her sister seemed to be permanently stuck in. In a year her parents would let her wear makeup, choose her own clothes, maybe even invite a boyfriend or two into the house, if she ever found a boy who wasn't a total dork.

The Hastings family had always operated like a clock or a calendar. When the clock said it was nine, you were on your way to bed. When the calendar said you were fourteen, you were allowed certain privileges, like staying up a half hour longer than your bucktoothed sister.

Once inside her room, Shawna stared into the mirror on her closet door. She was blossoming so fast that each peek into it brought new surprises. Today she discovered, after much searching, that she was developing a pimple under her nose.

Her breath came out in a slow sigh. Suddenly her reddish hair was a tangled rat's nest, her eyes were far too close together—almost comically so—and her small face was a breeding ground for pimples. She was becoming ugly—no, more than ugly: pukey. She would never have to worry about bringing boyfriends home because her ghastly face would scare them all away.

She raised one arm and sniffed her armpit through her pajama top. Seemed okay, nothing that would fell a tree. She pressed her hands to her chest and yes, things were definitely getting larger there. But her nipples hurt sometimes, so she probably had breast cancer and could kiss the whole disaster of her short life good-bye anyway.

Resigned to her fate, but not really believing any of it except the onset of pimples, she flipped the light off. She was asleep in ten minutes.

One hour later, Shawna's father, Jerry Hastings, got up from the living room couch, tossed his magazine—*Restaurant Management Review*—onto the coffee table, and raised his arms in a long, spine-cracking stretch. He followed it with a yawn. "I suppose I ought to go to bed," he said to his wife, Margaret.

Jerry was a six-year veteran of the restaurant wars, currently the assistant manager of a downtown Denny's. It wasn't exactly the Ritz, but he was close to promotion and a restaurant of his own, if things went right. Managing restaurants was a hard and thankless job, but the pay was getting better. Jerry had only a high school diploma and counted himself lucky not to be digging ditches or washing cars. At thirty-three, he knew no better job would ever come his way.

He nudged his wife with a foot and got kicked at for his trouble. She was deep into a rerun of "Night Court," laughing at the antics of her favorite character, Dan Fielding. Too bad Jerry's thermostat wasn't set on Permanently Horny, like Dan's. Yeah, their sex life was okay, he guessed, but he put in almost seventy hours a week at work and was usually too tired for anything but a slam-bam-thank-you-ma'am before he rolled over and dozed off.

"Just as soon as the show's over," Margaret said to the TV.

Jerry wandered up the stairs without complaint, shedding his clothes as he went. After a moment the hallway light snapped off and she heard the bed creak. Then: snores.

Margaret nodded to herself. He was as predictable as an avalanche when the snow got heavy. She stretched out on the sofa, lying on her side with her head resting on one hand, the flickering light of the television bathing her face in blues and reds. Within a minute her eyes began to droop. Within another she was asleep, snoring lightly herself, while the sitcom ended and the credits rolled to announce that yes, Reinhold Weege was still the producer.

Pocketknife's real name was anybody's guess. At age twenty he had flunked out of so many schools and been in jail so many times that even his parents preferred not to let his real name be known. Flynn, on the other hand, carried the first name Osgood, so his use of the last was understandable. Pocketknife was a product of the mean streets; Flynn had had to work hard at screwing his life up. Also twenty, he came from a stable, respectable family, and if it hadn't been for his drug use and his hostile attitude he might have become a doctor or lawyer. Instead he was a skinny, tattooed misfit with a fondness for cheap vodka and unfiltered cigarettes, and a penchant for stealing hood ornaments from expensive cars.

Pocketknife's car was a battered old Chevy Caprice that had no muffler on the pipe and no tread on the tires. It made a hellacious racket, which he enjoyed, especially when drag racing along the suburban streets at night. He liked to look over his shoulder to watch the house lights pop on just after he roared past, liked to imagine a dozen telephones jangling in the local police precinct. Payback for a life of poverty, a life out of control. How handy that none of it was his own fault.

But he and Flynn were not out cruising tonight just for fun.

"Getting closer," Flynn murmured to him.

Pocketknife turned his head. In the glow of passing streetlights his earrings—three in one ear, five in the other—winked metallically. "How can you tell?"

Flynn tacked on a grin. "As you should know by now, one of superior intelligence such as I can see beyond the realm of normal eyesight." He squinted through the cracked, yellowed windshield. "Take a right."

Pocketknife turned right, frowning. "These houses all look the same to me, man," he said.

Flynn plucked his latest bottle of vodka—Russian Star, available in stores for only $4.85—off the ruined seat and plugged it into his lips. Vodka gurgled, sparkling and sloshing in the backglow of the headlights. "You see," he said as he put the bottle between his legs, "the Flynns are known for their amazing mental powers. My father, for instance, predicted the assassination of President Kennedy three days before it happened."

"Oh, sure," Pocketknife said with a sneer. "What was he, about five years old then? Pretty smart kid. Pretty bad lie, too."

Flynn was, at times, an unbearably snotty little prick, especially when he was drunk, like now, but Pocketknife had few friends and had to hang on to the one or two he could claim. Besides, their line of work, this business of kidnapping, well . . . it was a two-man job. Too damn scary for one man alone.

"Take a left here," Flynn said.

Pocketknife veered left, catching a glimpse of the street sign as he turned. Bramble and Forest Vine streets, Bramble heading on to the east, Forest Vine cutting to the north. "Pass the bottle," he said after the turn.

Flynn held it up, still half full. "You gotta say please, man."

"Screw you."

"That doesn't sound like a please."

4

"Screw you, please. Gimme the goddamn bottle."

Flynn jerked up taller in the seat. "Take a left! Quick!"

Pocketknife cut a sharp left. The elderly tires squealed out a brief complaint.

"No wait! Right!"

Pocketknife cranked the wheel hard. The front left tire caught the curb and the old Caprice lumbered over it like a groaning dragon.

"No! Straight ahead!"

Pocketknife jammed the brakes on, bringing the car to a dead stop in the intersection, one rear tire still on the sidewalk. He whirled. "Cut it out, shithead! Gimme that freakin' bottle!"

Doubled up with laughter, Flynn handed it over. Pocketknife took a long, fiery drink and passed it back with a growl. He scuffed at his lips with his wrist, frowning and unhappy. Goddamned brainy idiot. Someday he was going to land both of them in jail. Again.

"Don't blow a hemorrhoid," Flynn cackled. "Just stop at any old house and we'll see what's inside."

In the meantime the car had died. Pocketknife cranked it alive and took off in a cloud of blue exhaust, wondering if that left front tire might be going flat now. He was making pretty decent money on these little midnight jobs and it just might be time to invest in a set of Road Handlers.

"This one will do," Flynn said after a moment.

Pocketknife slowed, craning his neck to look at the house ahead on the right. It was a white two-story dream house right out of a catalog. He was struck suddenly with the thought that they should move on, find another house, leave these people alone. The nightmare he and Flynn brought—and they had brought it to this area a few times before—was not something he had ever thought he could do. Sure, all he could get in this world was maybe a job pumping gas, and sure, the people inside that stately house probably had their good fortune handed to them on a platter, but did that give him the right to do what he was going to do?

"I don't like the looks of it," he said.

Flynn turned. "Huh?"

"This house. It don't look right."

Flynn frowned at him. In the poor light the snake tattoos on his biceps seemed to move and twist below the cuffs of his ratty white T-shirt, the one that read "Mensa Material." Whatever Mensa was, Pocketknife suddenly wanted no part of it. He pushed on the accelerator.

"No, stop!" Flynn barked. "This is the one!"

Pocketknife stopped. He hung his head, battling the vodka in his stomach that now wanted to rise to his throat. What did it matter? This house or that? In the end they were all the same, and the people in them might wind up dead.

"Cut the engine," Flynn whispered, and Pocketknife did. "Let's roll."

They got out and looked around. Some of the houses still had lights on, but not this one. A light breeze had sprung up, and Pocketknife shivered. He leaned back into the car, retrieved the vodka, and gulped some down. No way could he do this sober, or even half sober. It was just too weird.

"Christ, don't suck all of it down," Flynn hissed. "Come on."

Pocketknife tossed the bottle through the open window and followed. The booze seemed to sit in his stomach like an anvil, doing no good for his disposition at all. He decided, as he crept along behind Flynn, that tonight's job would be the last one for him. He would get a real job pumping gas, and Flynn could find another wheel man.

They came to a double row of hedges. Flynn signaled a stop, and they crouched there, taking a final look. Ornate front door, large picture windows with drapes drawn inside, an actual birdbath in the center of the lawn. "Looks good," Flynn whispered above the rush of the rising breeze that was rippling his T-shirt into crazy, spooky shapes as he knelt there. "No dog, at least. Not outside, anyway."

He dug through the grass and found a pebble. He

tossed it hard against the middle picture window. *Ping!* Then another. And then he waited.

No dog barked inside. Not perfect proof that no man-eating Fido lived here, but better than nothing. "Let's go," he said, straightening up. Pocketknife stood behind him looking sick and fevered.

The porch light snapped on.

"Oops!" Flynn grunted, and they both dropped into the safe darkness behind the hedge.

Pocketknife's breath began to pick up pace. They waited for five minutes, ten. Each one was as long as eternity to him, as if time had slowed down to give him a lengthier opportunity to hate himself and what he was becoming. After a few more interminable minutes the light went out.

Flynn turned his head to look at him, grinning. "Motion detector," he whispered. "That's all."

He started to rise, but Pocketknife snapped a hand out and caught the tail of his Mensa shirt. "What if there's an alarm hooked to it?"

Flynn jerked away. "Then we'll find out, won't we? Get your ass in gear."

Pocketknife rose and followed him to the steps of the stately front porch. The porch light immediately sprang alive, casting long, threatening shadows across the lawn. Flynn crept up and touched the doorknob.

They waited for the alarm while the breeze played through the hedges behind them and made the branches scrape softly against each other, sounding to Pocketknife's ears like a hangman's noose rubbing against the skin of the condemned man's neck. His heart was hammering and his breath felt like an acid mist as it slid in and out of his lungs. In a pocket of his Levi's was his knife, the one he had found in an alley when he was seven. Five times in his life it had been wet with human blood. When this night was over, his interior voice vowed, the damn thing was going straight into the river.

Flynn leaned against the door with his hand still on the knob. A strange smile of anticipation touched his lips, and in his eyes Pocketknife could see a sheen of glee. Or madness. Or of simple, boyish joy. Flynn pulled a short butcher knife out of his back pocket, his weapon of choice. It was eleven o'clock.

He drew back and slammed himself into the door. The jamb split neatly apart and the door swung open. Flynn groped along the wall, and a moment later the room was bathed in light from a ceiling fan. The fan began lazily to turn.

Pocketknife followed him inside, sick, quaking. The house smelled of many dinners cooked and eaten, of air freshener and furniture polish, of coming disaster. He saw with a burst of shock that a very sleepy woman was rising up from the sofa, looking the other way. *Run!* he wanted to scream, but although he might not starve without his pay from these missions, he would suffer. Clothes, booze, his burgeoning cocaine habit, a few bucks for a movie or a carnival—for these luxuries he needed money. Although he lived at home with his nine brothers and sisters and the food stamps were ample, he was too old to be a dependent and did not qualify for them. He often wished his brothers and sisters would all die, and maybe his mother too, because she was a slut; and then, for good measure, he often wished he would die as well.

All of this flashed and dimmed inside Pocketknife's head in the space of a heartbeat. He watched as Flynn scurried over to the woman, watched as he jerked her head back and raked the butcher knife across her throat even as she squawked in surprise. When he let her go she began to walk around in small circles with one hand pressed against the gaping red grin in her throat and the other clawing at the air that smelled so fine. Blood flooded down the front of her blouse in a crimson waterfall. Her severed larynx clicked and scraped as she struggled to breathe. At the sofa again she lost her balance and fell across it to soak the cushions with the blood that remained in her body. Her feet twitched, and one pink slipper fell off.

"Oooky!" Flynn said, his voice shaking with excitement, his eyes as shiny and hard as jumbo marbles. His mouth hung open.

Pocketknife turned his head and slapped one hand over his eyes, but still the woman made awful noises as she died.

"You!" Flynn shrieked.

Pocketknife heard his feet thumping across the floor. He pulled his hand from his eyes and saw that a man in pale blue pajamas had come out of a room at the head of the stairs and was looking down, his eyes huge with fright and confusion. Flynn charged up the stairs and stuck his knife neatly into the center of the man's stomach. With a jerk he rammed it up to the juncture of the man's solar plexus. A gray snake of intestine spilled out in a large loop and began to unwind to the floor.

Pocketknife dropped to his knees and vomited on the very nice gray carpet, tasting hot vodka and this evening's supper, two double cheeseburgers from the McDonald's on Elssely Street, some french fries, a Dr Pepper without ice. It all came up in a series of huge blurts that squeezed his stomach like a vise.

"Come up and check the rooms," Flynn barked, finding the hall light switch and flicking it up. "I'll see who else might be around."

Pocketknife wobbled to his feet. The world spun in a slow circle.

"Come *on!*"

He stumbled up the steps on his hands and knees, his long greasy hair dangling in front of his eyes, the knife burning a hole in his pocket and in his soul. At the top he got dazedly to his feet and lurched toward the nearest door, which was slightly ajar. He pushed through it, and in the dim light saw a girl sit up in bed. She had shoulder-length golden hair, mussed now from sleep.

"Get under the bed," he croaked. "Fast."

She was too terrified to move. Pocketknife backed out and swung the door shut until the latch clicked, then turned and pressed his back to it. Flynn reappeared from

9

another room and stalked toward him. "They gotta have a kid or two," he said in the clipped, self-assured tones of a man in control. "What's in there?"

Pocketknife swallowed with effort. "Nothing," he grunted. "Laundry room."

"Damn." Flynn thumped down the hall to another door, this one on the left. Please be empty, Pocketknife groaned to himself. For God's sake, please.

Flynn pushed the door open. The light came on. He turned suddenly and smiled at him. "I believe," he said, "that we have found what we're looking for."

Pocketknife's knees came unhinged, and he slid down the door onto his haunches. He watched through dull, deadened eyes as Flynn manhandled a screaming girl out of the bedroom. Her hair was reddish blond, her face pale and contorted. With a jerk he ripped her pajama top open.

"Looks like fresh meat to me," Flynn said. "Hey, girlie, feel like having the time of your life?"

She only screamed and fought. Even when Flynn backhanded her, hard enough to knock her jaw sideways and maybe crack some teeth, she continued to fight, though a line of blood, a horrible barn-paint red against the paleness of her skin, tracked from a corner of her lips to her chin.

She kept screaming as Flynn hauled her down the stairs, clamped a hand over her mouth, and forced her out into the night.

Pocketknife followed on legs that were scissoring and jerking. Mission accomplished. For tonight, anyway.

It was just past eleven.

CHAPTER

2

The Interrogation

Not again! Julie Hastings thought.

The door of her private hospital room, which smelled like Listerine, had swung open a few seconds earlier, and into the room—an artwork of white-on-white, white curtains at the window, white sheets, white walls—had walked police detective Sam Weatherspoon for just about the billionth time.

"Again?" she groaned as he settled himself into the white plastic chair beside her bed. For the last few days she had lain here, the monotony broken only by the pain of her burns and that damned whirlpool bath they made her sit in while a doctor plucked at her burned skin with tweezers—what did they call it? Dermatage? Dermabrasion? Whatever it was, it was painful.

She was glad, though, to be in as good shape as she was. Her last memory of that awful night, when she had chased Peyton and been waylaid by that horrible little madman, was of being doused with gasoline and set on fire. The rest was as blurry as the water swirling in the whirlpool tub. She remembered flopping in someone's arms, remembered being put down in front of a huge set of glass doors, remembered hearing some kind of buzzer being beaten to death. And then her rescuer had loped off into the night while an orderly and a nurse—her first indoctrination into the world of white—came out and placed her on a stretcher and hurried her into the emergency room.

"So how are you doing today?" Detective Weatherspoon asked, propping one ankle on his knee and leaning back in the chair. He seemed genuinely concerned. A tall and amiable man, he had bright green eyes full of curiosity and wore a small mustache that twitched whenever he warmed to a subject or picked up a new clue. And he liked Julie's subject most of all, obviously, but her clues had so far been disappointing.

"I'm not dead yet," she answered, scooting herself up a little higher in the bed. She had resigned herself to looking like walking death in front of this handsome cop. Her face was smeared with burn cream, and white gauze covered the areas that had taken the brunt of the heat. There were no third-degree burns on her face, fortunately. The most severe damage had been confined to her back.

Detective Weatherspoon smiled. "Good. Has anything new come to you yet?"

She shook her head, rustling her hair against the pillows that were propped against the headboard. Why did he insist that she remember things? The whole ordeal was better left forgotten, for her sake, anyway. She could understand, however, that the cops wanted answers. But she knew the little madman was dead—spectacularly dead, his head ripped off and tossed into a gutter—and the mysterious case of the man who burned women at the stake was closed. But still the police wanted more.

They wanted to know who had decapitated the madman without so much as a knife or a hatchet. Had she seen him? Could she describe him? Would returning to the scene of the crime jar her memory? No, thanks, I think I'll just get on with my life. As soon as I get out of this damned hospital, that is.

"We picked up some new evidence," Weatherspoon said casually. "Nothing spectacular, sadly, but at least it's something."

She frowned. Big deal. "You found out the little creep's name?"

He shifted in his chair. "Actually, no. You were the third woman to burn, but not the only person he burned without benefit of a stake. A psychiatrist and his receptionist were also killed the way you almost were. A jar of gas, a match or lighter. Probably a match."

"My guy used a Bic," she said.

"I know. The point is, the guy was obviously a nut. We're still trying to get that shrink's files opened, but the courts have to decide if doctor-patient confidentiality would be violated if we screened all the records. If I could get my hands on those files, or on the tape recorder he used in his sessions, I'd be a happier man."

She smiled without much humor. "Doubtless."

He regarded her with a frown. "You don't much like me, Julie, do you?"

"I just hate answering the same questions all over again."

"Okay, then," he said, "I'll ask some new ones. How did your fiancé die?"

She jerked. "Pardon?"

"Peyton Westlake. You two were engaged about two years ago, but he was killed. Correct?"

Julie's mind shifted into sudden confusion. What could Peyton have to do with this? She knew he was alive, but no one else did. And if he wanted his whereabouts to be kept secret, she was not going to deny him that wish. "Peyton died in a laboratory explosion," she said evenly.

"So I've gathered. Did they ever find his body?"

"Just one of his ears," she said.

"But they did recover the body of his lab assistant."

"Yes."

Weatherspoon took a breath, thinking. "What kind of man," he said slowly, "would have the strength to tear another man's head completely away from his body? With his bare hands, mind you. The coroner was very certain of this, but also very mystified. He says it is physically impossible."

She shrugged. "So?"

"So this: have you ever heard of a medical process known as the Rangeveritz procedure?"

She didn't need to think at all. "No."

"It's quite interesting. It's an operation in which all of the pain sensors of the external body—the skin—are severed. The purpose is to eliminate the pain of terrible wounds, such as the severe abrasion a motorcycle rider would get after falling off the bike and sliding a few hundred feet on his back. Skin wounds that massive hurt like hell. Ever had a rope burn?"

She shook her head.

"I did once," he said. His mustache twitched, and he uncrossed his legs to lean closer. "I got into mountain climbing some years ago—I know, I know, there aren't any decent mountains around here. In fact at that time I lived in Colorado, just west of Denver. One time I started to fall. It wasn't far and the worst I might have gotten was a sprained back or broken arm. But I panicked, as most people do when they start to fall, and I grabbed my partner's guy rope with both hands. He had already driven his piton into a crack, so the rope held." He raised his hands, palms outward.

Julie almost gasped.

"Pretty wicked rope burn," he said, watching her. "Hurt like nothing else I've ever gotten, even more than the broken arm I got in that same fall. Imagine having a burn that severe over most of your body."

She snorted. "I have no trouble imagining that at all."

He dropped his hands. "What you have is child's play compared to what you could have gotten. Ever seen a human being who's been *really* burned? I mean *really!* The pain is so excruciating that it cannot be alleviated, even with morphine or Demerol. So a doctor named

Rangeveritz comes up with a new idea, and immediately over thirty people across the country are having their nerves severed. Neat, huh?"

She thought of Peyton. He had been worse than burned; he had been skeletalized. Had they used the Rangeveritz procedure on him?

"But then," Weatherspoon went on, "like many other drastic new medical discoveries, came the darker side of the story. A side effect, of sorts. Every single one of those patients went mad."

Julie blinked. "Mad?"

He nodded. "Yeah. Not mad like angry, but mad like insane. Some of them committed horrible crimes. Others committed suicide. More than a few are in straightjackets right now, bouncing off the walls in rubber rooms, as insane as rabid dogs."

She felt her internal temperature drop a few degrees. That would explain Peyton's bizarre behavior over the last two years. But insane? Peyton insane? Impossible. He was too smart to ever go crazy. "Detective Weatherspoon," she said, "what in the world could this *possibly* have to do with Peyton Westlake? He has been dead for two years. There is a tombstone at the Greenlawn Cemetery with his name carved on it. I often put flowers there."

He spread his hands, and again she caught the sight of those ugly Freddy Krueger–style scars. "Let's just call this a conversation between friends, then. Did you know that about two miles downstream from your fiancé's former laboratory is a hospital? It's not exactly on the riverbank, I'll admit, but it is close. According to their records—medical records are not as hush-hush as psychiatrist's are—a severely burned John Doe was brought to the hospital by two fishermen who'd found him on the bank. The docs performed the Rangeveritz procedure on him. A day later he escaped by snapping his leather wrist and ankle restraints and diving through a second-story window."

Julie's throat felt suddenly dry, as dry as ash.

"No normal human being could have done that, Julie, but a man who'd undergone the Rangeveritz technique could. One effect of that radical procedure is an extraordinary output of adrenaline that gives the victim almost superhuman strength, enabling him to bend steel bars and the like. Since the cutting of nerves would leave our John Doe with little external feeling, he wouldn't mind getting his wrists all cut up and bruised. The fifteen-foot drop to the ground didn't faze him. A very dangerous man, in other words."

He looked at her speculatively, tapping his knee with a finger. "The kind of man, let's say, who could rip another man's head off in a fit of rage and toss it into the gutter."

Julie let her eyes slide shut. What was going on inside her had to stay hidden; a storm was brewing in her mind that Weatherspoon must not see. "A very creepy story indeed," she said as levelly as she could. She faked a yawn. "These pain pills are making me sleepy," she said. "Could we call a halt to this until, say, a few years from now?"

"Or tomorrow," he retorted.

"Or tomorrow. Whenever. Just no more today, okay? No more."

He stood and smiled. "It seems to me," he said amiably, "that if Peyton Westlake were still alive, he would come to you first. And if you were in trouble—say, on fire or the like—he would certainly try to rescue you. Even if he had to rip a man's head off to do it."

"Good-bye," she said coldly.

He turned, took a step, turned back. "Incidentally, Julie, do you know how your rescuer put out the fire that was about to kill you?"

"I have no memory of that," she said.

"It took us a while, but we finally pieced it together. Whoever saved you hosed you down with human blood. The headless man's blood. Squeezed the blood out of the corpse like water out of a balloon. He put out the fire and carried you eighteen blocks before vanishing. Strong fellow, don't you think?"

She was suddenly angry—angry at a world that would turn Peyton into a freak, angry at the cop who was playing guessing games with her. "You know," she said, barely able to keep that anger out of her voice, "I would think you'd be grateful to the man who killed that serial murderer, instead of trying to hunt him down like a criminal. After all, how many more people might he have burned alive? How many before your police force could have done what one man did all by himself? *I* was the one on fire, and *he* was the one who saved my life. I don't care whether he was Jesus Christ, Jack the Ripper, or Quasimodo, *he* saved me. *You* didn't. So get out of here and go chase down some real crooks."

Weatherspoon's mustache twitched again. "You still love Westlake, don't you?" he said, and didn't even try to dodge the pillow she hurled at him as he left.

But he was back in less than ten minutes.

"What now?" she said icily as he came in.

"I'm afraid," he stammered, "I'm afraid . . ."

She sat up straight, alarm flooding her mind. Weatherspoon looked genuinely ill, and he was not the type of man to either look ill or mince words. "Afraid of what?" she asked.

He took a breath. "We've just found the bodies of a man and woman who were murdered in their home. One little girl is alive. The other one is missing. That's what I've just been told. I'm sorry to bring this kind of news."

"What do you mean?" she nearly shouted. "What does that have to do with me?"

His Adam's apple jumped as he swallowed. She had never noticed before just how big his Adam's apple was. But it was bobbing up and down in his neck like a kid on a pogo stick.

"Tell me!" she demanded. "Tell me!"

He jerked his head. "The victims were your brother

17

Jerry and his wife, Margaret. They're both dead. Your niece Shawna has been kidnapped. Only the younger girl is left, Tina."

"What?" she cried. "What!"

And for the first time in her life, whether from the weeks confined to a bed or from the shock, Julie fainted dead away, hitting her head on the headboard but feeling nothing at all.

CHAPTER

3

Special Delivery

Norman Hopewell stood at a rear window in his large home north of the city, sipping brandy from a large snifter. He had been known some years ago to the viewers of station KMXT in Arizona as the host of "An Evening with Reverend Hopewell and God," a local TV series that focused more on raking in donations than on religion. After serving eight months at the Cromwell minimum-security prison in Yuma for tax evasion and fraud, Hopewell had moved to the Midwest and tried to go straight. For a while. Being a high school dropout whose only talent was the ability to lie well, he had found that construction work, burger-slinging, and corn-shucking—three jobs he'd held for a few days—were not quite his style. Possessed of an enormous ego, he felt driven to be a leader of men. And the best way to do it, he had decided, was to open a church and start passing the plate.

But now that his new church was firmly established, he was worried. "Freaking low-life punks," he muttered to himself. Standing at the window of the darkened room at the back of his mansion, he was waiting for the arrival of his henchmen, Pocketknife and Flynn. In the living room music was thundering, rattling the windows, and many feet were stomping, many hands clapping. Tonight's service was in full swing. At midnight the faithful expected a show. If Pocketknife and Flynn failed to show up with the goods, there would be no spectacle, and the faithful, all forty-two of them, would be bitterly disappointed. Disappointed enough, maybe, to quit the flock. And that would be the end of Hopewell's new career as high guru. Without his followers he could not afford his huge mortgage payments; without them he would be back at McDonald's flipping burgers, with the teenage employees snickering behind his back at the forty-year-old dude without a pot to piss in. It had happened before.

"Come on, come *on!*" he said to himself, fogging the window with his breath. He checked his watch: eleven-thirty. Shit. If there was no virgin to be defiled tonight, it would be good-bye, flock. Maybe his followers were already shedding their clothes, putting on their robes, getting ready for the midnight march to the guest cottage and the real fun. The spotlights there were already lit, the altar banked with the candles necessary for the Ceremony of Youthful Defilement.

Hopewell was suddenly aware of someone behind him in the darkened room. He spun around, a snarl curling his lips.

It was only Fritz, dressed as usual in his shabby mail-order suit. Fritz was Hopewell's bodyguard and the second-in-command of this new cult of old folks and idiots. "Are they out there yet?" he whispered to Hopewell. Fritz clasped a bottle of rum in his right fist, a cigarette in his left. Hopewell had never known any man who could put away as much liquor as Edgar P. Fritz. The fat little man could polish off a keg or two of beer and still be on his feet. Amazing. Too bad he was not blessed with the gift of gab; drunk or sober he found it hard to speak to groups. If he'd had talent, Norman Hopewell could have sat back and taken it easy while Fritz did the work. As it was, Hopewell's voice got hoarse after an hour or two of preaching. Fortunately the flock assembled only on the fourth Friday of every month for the dancing and the revelry, and of course the defilement; otherwise, Hopewell would have had tired vocal cords *all* the time.

"No," he whispered back, "they aren't here yet. God-damn sleazy punks. Why did you hire them in the first place? You can't trust punks like them."

Fritz drew up beside him, reeking of booze and tobacco, and looked out the window at the expanse of lawn that ended in a stand of brush and scrub trees. In that little glen there must soon appear a pair of head-lights and an old Chevy Caprice with a virgin in the back—or at least a young girl, to hell with her virginity or the lack thereof—or the defilement was off. "How many other fools," Fritz said, "would take that kind of risk for fifteen hundred dollars apiece, your royal high-ness? What did you expect for that kind of money—a professional mafia hit man? We're lucky I found them, reliable or not."

Hopewell set his brandy down and wagged his head. "God help us if we disappoint the flock. They paid good money to see a defilement, and I don't give refunds. How's the party going, anyway?"

Fritz chuckled, a low, rumbling sound that rose from his ponderous belly like an attack of gas. "The old farts are dancing their asses off. It's a miracle five or six of them haven't keeled over dead from a heart attack yet." He raised his bottle of rum to his lips. Gurgle. Gurgle. Hopewell watched him with both disdain and amaze-ment. What kept the little fat man's liver going?

Hopewell turned to the window again. In the darkness outside a brilliant slice of moon was trying to rise in the east, casting long, fuzzy shadows over the lawn and its assemblage of concrete statues. The statues had been in place when he bought the house: twelve prancing mythi-cal figures reminiscent of ancient Greek and Roman paganism, satyrs and gorgons and dragons, each about three feet high. One of the reasons he'd decided to live here was those statues. Searching for a new angle, a new scam, he had been reminded of the old classical mythologies. Then it had come to him: the Church of Eternal Youth and Beauty, one goal of the ancient pagans. Corny at first, it had captured his imagination as he thought of the people who might be willing to join such a church. Old people, of course. And who had all the money nowadays? Not the kids or young adults, he knew. They were still struggling to establish themselves. It was the old grandpas and grandmas who had cash to burn. Especially in this ritzy, secluded area overlooking the city, where the houses were hills apart and the privacy was almost complete.

Light caught his eyes; twin headlight beams speared the sky and splashed off the greenery. Pocketknife and Flynn at last. Relief washed through Hopewell in a pleasant wave. The faithful would not be disappointed on this night of youthful defilement.

Fritz set his bottle on a table, stabbed his cigarette out in the ashtray there, then straightened. "I'll handle it from here," he said. "You go prep the flock."

"Hold on a second," Hopewell said, snatching at his sleeve. "First we have to make sure they got a girl. If I tell the faithful to line up for the march and there's no virgin in the guest cottage, we're dead in the water." He squared his shoulders, rising to his full height of five feet four inches, one good inch taller than Fritz, whom he considered a dwarf, and a fat one at that. Hopewell's hair was thick and black, his face a nondescript pale oval jeweled with lackluster eyes, a large flat nose, and a mouth that tended to hang open when he was thinking hard.

He and Fritz left the room together, stepping out into the hallway, then hurrying down it to the living room of the house. The party was at its apogee, crazy lights strobing and flashing, the smell of booze and marijuana thick in the air. The stereo with its ceiling-high speakers was thundering out a heavy-metal number, something by the Scorpions or Guns n' Roses—Hopewell did not know or care which. He had simply stocked up on the most abrasive CDs he could find.

Gathered together in the noise and mayhem of this cathedral-size room were the members of his faithful flock, forty-two doddering old men and sagging old women dancing and swaying to the beat, howling, laughing, sweating. To remain youthful you have to *act* youthful, that was the message of the Church of Eternal Youth and Beauty. These geriatric losers were afraid enough of old age and death to buy this eternal youth crap. Hopewell found it hard to believe that they really *did* believe all his lies. Once a month they got together to party and swing and screw, and for this privilege they paid a mandatory monthly tithe of sixteen hundred dollars. In reality—or at least in Hopewell's opinion—what they really came for was the monthly defilement. A revenge upon a representative of the young who had usurped them, captured their fading youth and made it their own while the old people dwindled away into their sixties, their seventies, their eighties, and the certain death that followed. Hopewell pushed through this crowd, nodding and smiling as they made way for him with love in their eyes. The smell of sweat and perfume was as thick as steam over a hot swamp.

He came to the patio doors and waited for Fritz to work his way through the crowd. Across the lawn now lay only moon shadows and darkness. In that darkness, if God was in his heaven and all was right with the world, was a battered old Caprice with two idiots and a virgin inside. Glad to get out of the noise, Hopewell slid the door open and stepped outside. Fritz followed.

Crickets were chirping; off in the woods birds were cawing out a good-night, ceding to the darkness and the mysterious night bugs that screeched and buzzed until dawn. Hopewell strode across the lawn with a light sweat cooling his forehead, Fritz scurrying behind him. Skirting those fascinating statues, Hopewell made his way to the edge of his property and found the Caprice at the head of an old country lane that had been unused for years, but was now very convenient.

He bent to look inside. "Any luck?"

23

Pocketknife, visible only as a collection of earrings twinkling in the moonlight, seemed to be resting his forehead on the steering wheel. The motor ticked as it cooled, shedding its heat in waves that drifted around the car, smelling of exhaust and engine trouble. It occurred to Hopewell that this business of virgin-napping must be hard work.

"Yeah, we got a nice one," the other shadow said. "Click on the dome light, my man."

After a second the dome light sprang wearily to life. And there, lying on the back seat, crudely blindfolded, her hands bound with twine, and a rag stuffed into her mouth, was the girl. Hopewell's heart jumped into his throat and began to pulse heavily there. This one was a rare find indeed, a beautiful young thing with a mane of reddish blond hair and a small, cherubic face that was wet with tears. Her pajama top was open, exposing youthful breasts that were beginning to flower in earnest. He felt his breath grow hot in his lungs, hot enough to scorch. If he hadn't reached out suddenly to hook his fingers over the Caprice's rain gutter, he feared he might have fallen. Usually these punks brought in some scraggly teenager with acne, tattoos, and a surly attitude. Convincing the flock that trollops like that were virgins was a tough job. But not with this one. Hopewell wished suddenly that he were fifteen again. He would date this gem all the way to the altar.

The altar?

God in heaven, there was an altar in the guest cottage —actually a polished steel table he'd bought from a medical supply store—and upon that altar this virgin was scheduled to be defiled in about twenty minutes. Could he let that happen?

"Okay, toss her out," Fritz said.

Flynn popped his door open, got out, and leaned back in for the girl. He dumped her unceremoniously among the weeds and thistles, then grinned at Fritz. "Three thousand smackers in small bills," he said, and extended an open hand over the hood.

Fritz made an envelope appear from somewhere under his cheap suit coat and handed it across. "I counted it, so don't waste my time doing it again, at least until we're gone."

"Want us to wait?" Flynn asked, counting it anyway.

"As usual."

He looked up craftily. "We don't get paid enough to wait all night, you know."

Fritz snorted. "You'll wait for as long as it takes, sleazeball."

Flynn's crafty grin twisted into a snarl. "Don't go mouthing off at me, asshole."

Fritz jerked; in the moonlight he now held a small chrome pistol in one hand. "Asshole this, tattoo-boy. You and your partner sit tight with your mouths shut until it's over."

Flynn raised his hands a little. "Ease off, dude, ease off! We'll be here!"

"I thought so," Fritz said, and pocketed the gun. He turned his head to stare at Pocketknife. To Flynn he said, "What's the deal with your pal? Is he hurt?"

"Nah." Flynn eyed him, too. "He puked when I gutted this chick's old man. He's going soft on us."

Hopewell had wandered to the other side of the car and now tore his gaze away from the girl. He shot Flynn an evil glance that he doubtless could not see in the dark. "Don't tell me you killed somebody this time."

"Okay," Flynn said easily. "We didn't kill nobody."

"We don't pay you to murder people. Your job is to borrow a girl for a couple of hours and then dump her someplace. I don't want any blood spilled, and I sure as hell don't want to know if you kill somebody. Got me?"

"You're got, you're got. Relax, man, don't pop an artery."

Hopewell relaxed. Once again his eyes wandered to the girl, so young and so innocent and so pretty under the rising moon. Flynn got back in the car and shut the door. The dome light went out.

"Roll this piece of junk down the road a ways," Fritz said, motioning. "Nobody needs to see you."

Pocketknife recovered long enough to take the car out of gear. It rolled backward, crunching over sticks and leaves. About twenty yards down the hillside its brakes squeaked briefly, taillights flaring in the dark.

Fritz crossed to the girl and bent to pick her up.

"Hold on," Hopewell said, blocking him. He was sweating heavily now, his heart squeezing painfully inside his ribs and throat. The girl was a gem, a precious gem. An angel on earth. "Go tell the faithful that the defilement will be delayed a little. I need some time with her."

"No," Fritz said immediately. "I need time to get her prepped, get her into the tabernacle."

"The preparation can wait. Tell the flock that things have been delayed because we have an extra special virgin. They'll buy that excuse."

Fritz growled. "Dammit, Norm, you know that's not the way it's supposed to go!"

Hopewell whirled to face him, his face twisting with anger. "Who is the grand guru of this operation, Fritz? Who's supposed to give the orders?"

Fritz softened. "You are," he said. "But why do you . . ."

His voice trailed off. He looked at the girl moaning on the ground, looked at Hopewell. And then he knew. "She's supposed to be a virgin, Norm," he said, his voice dark and full of reproach.

"Who the hell will know?"

"It's not the right thing to do, Norm. You're breaking your own strict rules."

"I make the rules, I break the rules."

Fritz thought it over. His eyes were wide and shiny in the moonlight. "I'll tell you what," he said. "I'll do what you say, I'll even bring the holy robe out to you when you're done. But I have to say that this is getting weird, Norm. Too weird."

Hopewell laughed. "What do you think the monthly

defilement is—a church raffle? I'm the head honcho, so nothing's weird unless I say it is. And maybe this is a new part of the ceremony. The guru gets to test the girl's virginity before the official ceremony."

Fritz scratched his nose. "They might buy it."

"Hell, they don't even have to know it. I just need a few minutes. The gods of youth are directing me." He straddled the girl and began jerking at her pajamas.

Fritz turned away, grumbling. "Somebody needs to," he said under his breath, and strode away. Halfway to the house he heard the girl scream. It sounded like the squealing of a sacrificial pig. "Too weird," he muttered, and hurried to get away from the noise, not really understanding why he was troubled about it at all. A defilement is a defilement, whether performed by one man on the ground or twenty men on a steel table. Maybe he was going soft in the head.

He stepped inside to the lights and the blaring music and the shouting, yet still, impossibly, he could hear the virgin's screams.

CHAPTER

4

Darkman at Home

Peyton Westlake was at his huge home in the dead and rotting heart of the city. His home was the Reyton Soap Factory, which had been closed and abandoned for the better part of thirty years. It seemed that the consumers of the early 1960s were not very fond of Fresh Splash soap or anything else the factory put out, so the company had folded and the building had been put up for sale. By then, however, the entire central section of town was dying, and no one seemed interested in purchasing a proven loser. So there it sat, occupied for thirty years only by rats, bats, cats, and winos.

Then it had become Darkman's lab, where he could work on his artificial skin experiments, alone and unbothered. When the day came that the skin was perfected—when it would last a lifetime in the sunshine instead of the current ninety-nine minutes—he would become Peyton Westlake again, no longer a prisoner of the night. If, that is, the Rangeveritz procedure had not driven him completely insane by then.

Darkman was seated in the rusted remains of an office chair he had found in a Dumpster, his computers and equipment spread out around him on doors suspended from the ceiling by chains and made to serve as tables. A swinging lab, he liked to think. A tremendous earthquake could strike the city and his precious equipment—most of it salvaged from his blown-up riverbank laboratory after he escaped from the burn ward—would survive on these hanging tables.

Not that it mattered much. He still had a briefcase lying around here someplace with almost fifty thousand dollars in it. It was dirty money, stolen from the goons who had destroyed his face just a little over two years ago. The money had been intended as payment for a batch of cocaine, but Darkman had posed as the drug kingpin and intercepted it. Dirty money or not, it was very much needed. Darkman could hardly get a job in his condition. He had once, very briefly, toyed with the idea of getting work at an all-night restaurant, a twenty-four-hour Burger King, maybe. With luck the skin would last the night. But, he had reasoned, if some irate customer came to him howling that this milk shake was runny or the fries were cold, Darkman might fly into a rage and kill the bastard. That would get him fired, at the very least.

And so he used the dirty money. Anyone else would have done the same. Such moral dilemmas would have kept Peyton Westlake awake at night. The man known as Darkman had no time for such luxuries.

At this moment he was hunched over the charred husk of a microscope whose lenses had survived the fire, adjusting the focus to see clearly what he had already seen a thousand times over the years: the artificial skin cells. My, but they did look healthy, bouncing around like a spoonful of amoebas, the dark dots of their nuclei solidly formed and pulsing with vitality. For this experiment he had shut down the big Honda generator that was parked in a back room and which supplied all his juice. In darkness cut only by the microscope's tiny light, he watched for another moment, then pulled his eyes away and groped for the test tube of emulsion sitting in a rack there. The solution consisted of sterile water and a crushed vitamin pill with a dash of salt. In the last eight years he had tried all things scientific and proper to make the cells survive longer; now he was reduced to oddball concoctions like this one.

He stuck the tip of a pin into the solution and withdrew a tiny bead of it. He touched it to the slide in the microscope and looked back inside.

The cells were dead.

"Overdose," he muttered, and leaned back in his skeletal chair. What had he been thinking? Artificial skin cells had no more use for vitamins than a cheap wig had need for hair oil. The flaw was in the cells' basic structure. They had to be made impermeable to light. Artificial skin was no good at all if the patient had to stay in a closet all day long. But what could protect the cells from light?

He ground his bony knuckles into his eyes. On this afternoon, a hot one, he had forsaken the customary head wrapping of gauze and was instead bared for all the world—if the world happened to come tripping by—to see as he really was: a previously handsome man burned to the bone, his head a baked skull striped with charred muscles, his hands twisted bone. Someday, he supposed, the artificial skin would be ready for constant wear and he would be as good-looking as, say, Tom Cruise. Or Lawrence Welk. Or Dracula. Or the Elephant Man. In fact, he could be anybody he wanted to be. And wouldn't it be fun to masquerade as, maybe, the president? *Really* get him in trouble?

Darkman stood up suddenly, not amused by all of this. The skin experiment was another failure. He was no closer now than he had been three years ago. What did those cells need?

He was in a back room that had once been an office, getting the generator started up when it hit him— a dark tinting solution. Would that make them light-proof?

When the generator was roaring again and the lights were alive, he hurried to the Bio-Press, the machine that produced false faces and hands, and took up a smear of the skin solution on a Q-Tip. He dabbed it on a fresh slide and put it under the microscope.

Healthy cells, bouncing as they swam. Now for something dark to stain them with, something really dark, something black.

He started away from the table, then stopped in mid-stride. He had no black liquid around here, not even a bottle of shoe polish. Maybe some ink? But ballpoint ink was hardly a natural dye; it contained resin and alcohol. He needed food dyes—FD&C black number 27 or the like. But was there really a black food color? Well, if not, there ought to be. What made licorice black? How did bakers whip up black Halloween cookies? If no food coloring was available, he could make black dye on his own. Mix up red and green and blue and all the other happy colors of the rainbow and what do you get? Black, of course.

So he needed to go shopping. That meant preparing a new batch of skin, programming a face into the computer, and shaping the stuff in the Bio-Press—just to go down to the corner market, which in reality was about twenty-five corners away.

To hell with it, he decided. Black absorbed light anyway. It would probably make the cells go belly up twice as fast as their natural beige color did.

So then, what to do? This was becoming a real problem. As the creature known as Darkman he had little use for people, needed no company to disturb his solitude, was perfectly happy to be alone. A part of him was still the man Peyton Westlake, however, and that part needed some interaction with humanity. But the last time he had put on a face and stepped out for a drink, he'd wound up involved with some very shady characters and had nearly lost his life.

He touched his wound now with one hand. He had plugged the bullet hole up with artificial skin and slept for three days. Or tried to. The pain had been bearable but annoying. Now, a few weeks later, he assumed he was healed. He could only feel the wound when he stretched or yawned, a minor bother. The bullet had passed clean through him, thank God, so he had been spared the messy chore of digging it out with a spoon.

He wondered how Julie was doing. A self-taught expert on burns, he believed that she would bear scars only on her back. Her face had been cherry red from the heat, her hair fried in a few places, but there had been little real damage. She was still as pretty as she had been on the day he proposed to her.

He walked to the telephone—illegally hooked up to a pole outside—and picked up the phone book. In the Yellow Pages he found listings for the various hospitals in the city, including the Saint James where Julie was. Or at least where she had been. By now she'd probably been discharged and was back on the job. Fortunately the Rangeveritz procedure was illegal now, though he doubted the doctors would have done it to Julie anyway. Her burns were not as drastic as his own had been.

He started to dial the phone when it came to him that he had no idea what to say to Julie. She had once seen him as he really was, and he had decided to stay out of her life; she did not deserve to have a freak for a lover. But fate had stepped in and brought them together again. It seemed that, try as he might, he was destined to be a part of her life. So what was one little phone call between old friends?

He located the number again and dialed the phone. A receptionist answered immediately. "Patient information. How can I help you?"

He cleared his throat. He had not talked to a human being for weeks. "I have a friend who might still be in the burn ward," he said. His vocal cords had been toasted in the fire, and he knew that his voice was different now, harsher. "Her name is Julie Hastings."

Distantly, he heard a computer keyboard being pecked on. "Hastings, Julie S.," the woman said. "I can connect you."

"Wait," Darkman said, but the phone on the other end had already begun to ring.

Click. "Hello," Julie said. She sounded bad, very tired or something.

"Uh," he said. That didn't seem adequate, but it was about all he could think of.

"Hello?"

"Julie," he managed to croak. "This is . . . Peyton."

"Oh," she said. But what could he expect? He had run from her with her cries echoing down the empty streets. Had it not been for him she would not have been set on fire by that nut. She wouldn't even have been in the neighborhood.

"I'm sorry for what I put you through," he said. "How are you?"

Silence for a small jot of time. Then: "Jerry's dead, Margaret, too. Shawna was kidnapped." She began to cry. "Only Tina is left."

"Jesus," Darkman whispered. He did not know Jerry Hastings very well, but they had met several times and he'd seemed pleasant enough. Worked in a restaurant, if memory served him correctly. His wife was—had been —pretty. They had a couple of nice kids, too. When had this disaster struck? "Did they have a car wreck or something? I mean—no, it couldn't be that. Shawna was kidnapped?"

"She's the seventh girl in seven months."

He thought of his briefcase, the stolen money. "How much ransom does he want? I have some cash."

"No one's heard anything. The other girls all were released, but they had been . . . molested. Two of them are in psychiatric hospitals. Terrible things were done to them, but the police don't have a clue as to who the kidnappers are."

"Jesus," he said again. He noticed that the skin on his

arms was pebbled with gooseflesh. What a creepy world. "Is there anything I can do?"

She seemed to be calming down a little. "I don't know. I'm getting out of here today even if I have to jump out a window. Could we meet someplace?"

He deliberated, stunned by the pace of things. He had just wanted to ask about her condition, and now suddenly he was being drawn into a meeting. His first instinct was to say no. His second was to say yes. Julie would need all the help she could get to cope with this. "Sure," he said uneasily. "I can hike to the hospital, meet you there."

"When?"

"A couple hours?" He looked at his watch: one o'clock. "Say, about three? Will you still be there?"

"I'll wait for you out front. If I'm not there, look me up in room two twenty-seven."

"Okay." He realized that his heart was pounding. "Uh, Julie?"

"What?"

"Will it be hard for you if I show up as Peyton?"

A brief pause. "You *are* Peyton."

"I mean my face," he said. "If it's easier for you I can be someone else."

"Oh. Just be you," she said. "Isn't this strange, talking like this? I knew your synthetic skin was good, but I had no idea it was *that* good. You really can look just like someone else. Half the time I'm tempted to stop strangers on the street and try to peel their faces off to see if it's you underneath. Are you ever around me without my knowing?"

"Never," he said, but it was a lie. He had been several other people in her presence.

"Oh, God," she blurted suddenly. "I just remembered that you got shot. Are you okay? You sound a little out of breath."

"I'm fine," he said. "Minor nick. A Band-Aid took care of it."

"That's a relief. So I'll see you at three, right? Either outside or in my room."

"Got it," he said, and she hung up. He lowered the phone and looked at it. "I love you, Julie," he whispered to the dial tone, then shook his head to clear it, and got busy whipping up some new skin.

CHAPTER

5

The Betrayal

In the dead of night at a lonely mansion atop a hill where forty-two faithful believers were rocking and rolling to the beat of wild music, a phony preacher was falling in love.

In love?

No, impossible. The girl was shivering and sobbing on her bed of leaves and weeds, but yes, Norman Hopewell *did* love her, had perhaps waited all of his forty years for a girl like her. She was so young, so perfect. The judges and lawyers who said that it was illegal to love someone so young were not aware of the charm of a young princess like this. And hadn't girls back in the Renaissance, the time of, say, Romeo and Juliet, gotten married when they were about thirteen? There had been no law against it then, and there shouldn't be now.

Yet Hopewell could not quite understand the emotions that were rattling in his head so suddenly. Love was for fools and married men. Norman Hopewell could love only one thing, and that thing was made of paper and was green and could be spent. Hate was a more familiar feeling for him, the hate that he felt for people like his father and his mother, for the geriatric fools who believed his religious teachings, for the TV preachers who made millions of dollars. When Jim Bakker had fallen from grace, Hopewell had been overjoyed. When Jimmy Swaggart was caught with a prostitute—twice!—Hopewell had laughed until his face was wet with tears. That reaction was understandable. Norman Hopewell had once had dreams of being a rich and powerful man; he'd had dreams of being famous. In reality he was a failed small-potatoes TV preacher who had been caught doing what all the others did—lying and cheating and stealing—and he had gone to jail while most of the evangelical big shots did not. Hate and lies had guided his life. Until now.

He leaned down and kissed the girl on the lips. She gagged and jerked away. He ran his tongue into her ear. "I love you," he whispered into it, and worked his arm under her neck. He squeezed her, hoping that she would understand the depth of his new emotion, but she was stiff and shivering.

His partner, Fritz, appeared in the dark. He tossed a black robe on the ground beside him. "Are you done with her?" he asked coldly. "The faithful are getting into their robes."

Hopewell turned his face up to him, a face shadowed with anger. "Tell them to take a hike," he hissed. "Tell them the ceremony is off."

Fritz made a noise inside his nose. "Then kiss your ministry good-bye, Norm. I hope you can get unemployment benefits."

Hopewell worked himself up onto his feet. Leaves clung to his knees, and he swatted at them. "What's with you, anyhow? This whole scam is a crock, and the faithful are idiots. Go tell them that God told me not to have a defilement tonight. Say that God told me to wait for a sign or something. Tell them anything. Just leave me alone."

Fritz lunged suddenly and took two fistfuls of Hopewell's shirt in his hands. He jerked him close, practically nose-to-nose. "You're crazy, you know that?" he snarled. "I happen to make my living off this religious bullshit, too. Pull yourself together and start acting like a guru again or so help me I'll knock some sense into you!"

Hopewell tried to hit him, but his pedaling hands connected only with Fritz's shoulders.

Down the hillside, Pocketknife's door clicked open and his voice drifted up. "What's going on up there?"

Fritz pushed Hopewell away. "Mind your own business," he barked down the hill. He turned his attention back to his partner. "You listen up, Norm. You are going to do exactly what you do once every month, and that is to lead the flock in the Ceremony of Youthful Defilement. This girl is just one out of millions, and she'll be gone before morning. When we're rich enough, you can marry the freaking queen of England, but for now *we need a show!*"

"No show tonight," Hopewell grunted.

"Fine, then." Fritz released him. "No show tonight, and next month we can expect maybe four or five of the faithful to show up. We don't have a virgin now, so you want to cancel the whole service. Then maybe tomorrow or the next day one of the flock will feel pissed about spending his money for nothing, and he'll go to the cops. We'll both wind up doing time at the state pen. Is that the way it's going to be?"

"No defilement tonight," Hopewell said sullenly. "I love this girl."

Stunned and amazed, Fritz ground his knuckles into his eyes. "Have you completely flipped?" he said in a choked series of syllables. "We've defiled six other girls just like her. What does one more matter?"

"The others were pigs," Hopewell said. "Cheap sluts picked up by those two bozos you hired. This girl is a real virgin."

"*Was* a real virgin, Norm." He looked at his watch. "Time's running out," he said. "Are we having a defilement or not? Do we stay in business or do we go to jail?"

Hopewell bent and scooped the girl up. Weeds and

thistles were stuck to her pajamas, and he shook her to make them fall away. "You're a smart guy," he sneered. "Come up with a new angle, something the flock will like. Do whatever you have to, but this girl is mine."

Fritz toyed with the idea of simply getting his pistol out and shooting the kid. That would end all of this in a hurry. But then Hopewell, not the most stable mind in the world, might flip out and do something *really* stupid. "I think I've got an answer," he said as a sudden and very welcome brainstorm struck. "Norm, leave the girl here. I promise she won't be going anywhere. Get into your robe and lead the flock to the guest cottage. Tell them it's an extra special night, so don't get antsy. I'll take care of the rest."

"What rest?" Hopewell said gloomily.

"Don't worry about it. Just do what I said."

Hopewell put the girl down. "If she's so much as touched by those old perverts, I'll call the cops myself," he grumbled. "Nobody around here gets defiled until I say so."

"No problem," Fritz replied. This was all very strange —not just the stupid defilement or even the whole flock of morons who participated in it so gladly, but also Hopewell's sudden attitude change. Things appeared to be unraveling. He watched Hopewell work himself into the robe and stalk away.

Without a virgin, tonight's show would have to be changed. That was all too clear. The question was, what would be just as satisfying to the faithful? In the beginning they had sacrificed a few chickens on the altar in the guest cottage. They'd also tromped across some farmer's pasture looking for a cow to kill and mutilate. They had even handled snakes, whose fangs had been removed before Hopewell would even think of touching them. But up to now they had not performed the ultimate ceremony, the capper of them all.

They had never had a human sacrifice.

He drew his gun and started down the hill. Down there in the darkness were two humans, both of them highly expendable, both of them young. No one would ever believe they were virgins, but for this new addition to the roster of lunacies performed by the cult, maybe they didn't have to be. Hopewell, with his gift of gab, could explain it all and make it sound exciting.

A human sacrifice. Fritz shivered under his ill-fitting suit as he walked. Maybe—more than maybe—this was getting out of hand, but the money was good and crimes had been committed before. Besides, the penalties for kidnapping and for murder were pretty much the same, even though the kidnappings were only temporary and murder was permanent.

He got to the old Chevy and jerked a door open. Flynn's face loomed in the moonlight as he looked up, startled. Fritz stuck his pistol between his questioning eyes.

"You won't believe what's going to happen next," Fritz grunted at him.

Osgood Flynn, who'd been bullied by childhood enemies for his oddball name and his small size, found himself being bullied once more, this time not by kids but by a man known to him only as Fritz. The cool barrel of the gun pressed between his eyes felt as huge as a cannon loaded with power and death. "What's up?" he was able to mumble as fear sprouted in his stomach like a dark and poisonous tumor. "What's the deal?"

Fritz bent slightly. "Yo, Pocketknife," he said softly.

Pocketknife was a pair of big white eyeballs in the dimness. "Yeah?" His voice was shaking.

"You know that envelope full of money? It's all yours now."

"Yeah?"

"Yeah. Flynn, be a good boy and hand it to him."

Flynn took the money out of his pocket and passed it over, sitting stiffly while sweat began to trickle down his forehead. What the hell was up? They'd found a virgin, a real one this time, so everything should be kosher. Fritz and Hopewell should have taken her to the mansion atop the hill, done whatever they did with all the other girls, and brought her back for disposal at a very distant and deserted street corner. Six times before it had worked out that way.

Fritz pulled the pistol away slightly. "Get out."

Flynn got out, shaking and confused. His tattoos looked black as ink against the paleness of his sweaty arms as he shut the car door. "Don't let him do this," he said to Pocketknife. "Back me up here, man."

The money crackled as Pocketknife began to count it wordlessly. Fritz smiled, exposing straight white teeth where moonlight wetly sparkled. "Even in the dorky Midwest," he said smugly, "money talks and bullshit walks. Let's go."

Flynn considered his options. In view of the pistol and Pocketknife's sudden lack of interest in anything but the money, there seemed to be only one, and that was to obey. He assured himself that, yes, he was Flynn, the kid from the right side of the tracks who had made a long and difficult journey to the wrong side. He was tough and he was street-smart and he could not be killed, especially by a fat little man in a K mart suit with a shiny pistol in one fat hand. If things got any more tense around here, he just might have to relieve the man of his gun and bop him over the head with it a few times. That would show him.

Fritz shoved Flynn up the road. Looking up to the top, where the lights from the house penetrated the bushes, Flynn could see a lot of people through the patio doors, and Hopewell working his arms into his baggy robe. Flynn had seen the robes before, had seen people dressed just like that leave the house and file toward a smaller house to the left, where often the screams of the kidnapped girls rang out. Sometimes the people chanted; sometimes they joked and giggled as they stumbled drunkenly toward whatever business they had in the little house. Every month it seemed that more of them were there, most of them old and gray-haired under their hooded robes.

Flynn saw the girl he and Pocketknife had brought,

lying in the weeds softly moaning. Her eyes, wet and swollen with misery, met his and held them. Hopewell had done something to her, that much was obvious by the way her pajamas were wrenched apart, and Flynn didn't have to be a Fulbright scholar to know what had happened.

"That way," Fritz said, and nudged his spine with the pistol. Flynn turned to the left, his face folded into a frown, his eyes quick and darting. Could he make a break for it? Could Fritz track him in the dark with his little chrome peashooter? What would a bullet or two in the back feel like?

"In there," Fritz said behind him.

Flynn skirted the house that was so much smaller than the mansion, realizing now that it was larger than it looked. A family of three or four could live comfortably in it; the illusion of smallness was created by the nearness of the gigantic mansion. It struck Flynn that it was highly unfair for Hopewell to be so very rich. The man was a child molester and a master pervert. Unfortunately Flynn's own crimes had not been much more honorable.

He came to the front door and opened it, then stepped inside at Fritz's urging. He looked around sourly. Some construction had been done here recently. Walls had been removed to form one large room, a grand salon thickly carpeted with red pile that was missing in blocky lines where the walls had once stood. He wondered briefly if the roof would cave in without their support. His father had made his money in construction, so Flynn was not altogether ignorant when it came to carpentry. If the roof did collapse, he only hoped it would collapse when he was somewhere else.

Fritz prodded him farther inside. Flynn saw that there was some kind of operating table at one end of the room. A spotlight clumsily screwed to the ceiling was beaming harsh white light against the table's steel hide and reflecting in patterns on the remaining walls. The house smelled like plaster dust and sandalwood incense recently burned. A mystery to stump even a master detective, Flynn decided. The most disconcerting thing, though, the thing that made his breath hitch in his throat and his heart freeze in his chest, was that the table had straps. Thick canvas straps heavy with buckles that dangled to the red carpet. That table had been manufactured with some heavy-duty operating in mind. It occurred to him that Frankenstein had created his monster on a slab very much like this one.

"Get up on the table," Fritz ordered.

Flynn turned. "What's this all about? I didn't do nothing."

"Nobody said you did. Lie down on the table."

Flynn snorted. "I don't need my appendix out, fat man, and I sure as hell don't want a sex-change operation. *You* get on the freaking table."

Fritz took a large, weary breath. He motioned with the gun. "How about an instant lobotomy, bullet-style? You can make this either easy or hard."

Flynn bared his teeth in a sneer. "I choose hard."

Fritz lowered his hand slightly and shot him in the left thigh. The noise was unbelievably loud, considering the size of the gun, a huge pop that dwarfed that of any firecracker ever made.

Flynn grabbed his leg with both hands, unable to believe that blood was gushing between his fingers or that Fritz had had the balls to shoot him. Flynn's smart-ass, who-gives-a-shit way of approaching danger usually saved him when things got rough; this time it had earned him a hole in the leg.

"You son of a bitch!" he heard himself shriek.

"Get up on the table," Fritz said calmly, "or I'll perforate your other leg."

"All right, all right." Flynn hobbled to the table, still amazed that such a tiny gun could cause such huge pain, and sat on it with a grimace. The change in position seemed to make his leg bleed less; he relaxed his hands and examined the bullet hole. It was about the diameter of a pencil, and the blood pulsing out seemed to be slowing. No major artery hit, then. He would not have the unhappy chore of bleeding to death here.

"Lie down."

Flynn stretched out, grumbling to himself, and waited without much patience as Fritz strapped him to the table, jerking on the tethers hard enough to make the canvas groan and the buckles dig into his chest and stomach and ankles. He smelled booze on the fat man's breath as he worked. God, what Flynn would have given for one more chug out of his vodka bottle! As soon as this crap was over, he would go back to his boardinghouse and get screaming drunk. After that, he would hunt Fritz down and make some holes of his own.

Fritz stepped back. "Okay," he said without enthusiasm, then added to himself, "I hope to hell Norm can pull *this* one off. Idiot."

Flynn raised his head. With a little effort, he believed, he could work his hands out from under the straps, get his arms free, and tackle the buckles as soon as the fat man left. "I'm going to kill you for this," he said. "Long and slow."

"You're scaring me to death," Fritz muttered. He turned and walked out, pocketing his pistol as he went. He left the door open, which made Flynn wonder absurdly if mosquitoes would soon be dining on him as he lay sweating under the spotlight, but a moment later he heard something that chased away all other thoughts, even the thought of getting out of here and getting drunk and getting revenge.

People were coming. They were still far away and hard to hear, but they were coming nevertheless. Coming to the little house that seemed so big inside, where he lay strapped to a table straight out of a horror movie. They were coming for reasons he could not guess and that he never, ever wanted to know. He had been on this hill before—six times before—and he had heard the people file into this house, and later he had heard the girls scream. The screaming was bad, but right now, in retrospect, it did not seem so bad at all. What he was hearing now was worse, more ominous, more frightening.

They were coming. And as they came, he could hear them chanting.

CHAPTER

6

The Encounter

The day was warm and bright when Peyton Westlake arrived at the Saint James Hospital, a massive six-story limestone building with steel window casings. Squinting against the light, knowing that, after the long walk, he had little more than half an hour before his Peyton-face went up in smoke, he hurried up the shallow tier of steps, looking for Julie. For this outing he had worn jeans and a red T-shirt, had splashed a bit of Old Spice on his false face, and had shined his battered old scientist's shoes by rubbing them against the calves of his pants.

At the top of the steps the big glass doors swung automatically open, and he walked inside. The air conditioning, he realized, was in fine working order today, but nevertheless, this hospital, like all the others in the world, smelled of rubbing alcohol, antiseptics, and floor wax.

He located an elevator and was transported up to the second floor, where he set off down a corridor in search of room 227. Somehow he would comfort Julie, perhaps plugging himself back into the switchboard of her life to lessen the shock of losing her brother and sister-in-law.

Not to mention the kidnapping of her niece. If the kidnapper was true to form, however, Shawna would have been released by now, sexually molested and in shock, but alive. It is, he thought dismally as he found the right door, a tough world out there.

Before knocking, he hesitated, suddenly unsure of himself. Was this a good idea? Would he do more harm than good? He had sworn to himself that until the artificial skin was perfected he would not see Julie again. She had no need of the nighttime freak called Darkman. At least, not until today. Did she expect him to help find the kidnapper? Surely the cops were better in that sort of situation.

But then, not many cops could do what Darkman could do. No constitutional restraints or Miranda ruling could curb his actions. Just ask the man who had torched Julie.

It came to him that he did not want to think about that too much; the feelings were still uncomfortably strong—his rage at the lunatic who would have killed Julie, his remorse over having killed her attacker so horribly. Thank God that Julie had been too overwhelmed by fear and pain to notice how the fire was doused.

He rapped on the door and heard Julie sing out a come-in. Feeling strangely guilty, he pushed the door open.

She wasn't alone. A tall, slender man in an expensive-looking gray suit was seated at her bedside. It took several seconds for Darkman to recognize him, and then the memory returned in a quick mental flash: Martin Clayborne, local real estate developer worth several million bucks and earning more every day. A few weeks ago, disguised as someone else, Darkman had saved Clayborne's life.

Martin was holding Julie's hand. No handshake going on there, no sir. These two were strongly attracted to each other. For less than a second, less than the tiniest fraction of a second, Darkman wanted to kill him. Julie was his.

Instead he strode in, exuding false cordiality. Julie smiled at him, only smiled; he had expected, at the very least, a gasp of surprise at his reappearance from among the missing and the lost. Then he remembered that she was expecting him. Why else did they put telephones in hospital rooms?

"Peyton," she said. "Thank you for coming. Martin, meet Peyton Westlake."

Martin Clayborne stood up. He looked confused, but offered his hand. "Nice to meet you," he said. "Julie's told me . . . quite a lot about you. I hope I'm not intruding on a reunion." He looked at his watch. "I have a meeting soon anyway."

"Oh, don't go," Julie said.

Go, Darkman thought.

"I really have to be going," Martin said, hurrying out.

Darkman could sympathize: Julie had probably told him that Peyton Westlake had been hideously burned in a fire two years ago. For reasons of her own she had not mentioned the artificial skin, obviously. Why? Was she protecting his identity? Was the man of the dark a mild-mannered reporter by day? How silly.

"You look good," she said amicably, though her smile was faltering. "Just like you used to."

He went to her bedside. "I still haven't perfected the skin." The urge to hold her hand was strong. Instead he sat in the chair Martin had vacated. It still held a stranger's warmth. He checked his watch. A few minutes of visiting, and then back to the old homestead. No sense walking around in public with his face melting off.

"Ninety-nine minutes?" she asked.

"More in the dark."

She touched his shoulder. "Sorry. I hope you weren't embarrassed by Martin. He's such a sweetheart."

He dropped the subject. "How are the burns?"

"As good as gone, Peyton. They were fairly minor. Not like . . . yours."

He dropped that subject, too. "Any word yet about Shawna? Have they found her?"

Julie's face fell. "No, nobody knows anything. Six other girls were kidnapped over the last six months, and every one of them was found wandering around in a daze by the next morning. Did I tell you two of them are in psychiatric hospitals now?"

He nodded. "You did."

"Nobody's exactly sure what was done to them. Weatherspoon says they were blindfolded and molested by more than one person."

Darkman swallowed. A tough world indeed. "What's a Weatherspoon?" he asked her.

"Oh. Detective Sam Weatherspoon. He's the cop handling the investigation. He gives me the creeps."

"The bearer of bad tidings, huh?"

She nodded. "Bad, badder, baddest. I called Mom in Connecticut; she's flying in tomorrow. I've got to make funeral arrangements for Jerry and Margaret sometime today, see about their life insurance, find out if they left a will—a million other horrible things."

She clutched his hand suddenly. Tears began to swim in her eyes. "Can you believe it, Peyt? Jerry murdered, Margaret, too, Shawna kidnapped and little Tina an orphan? It's like a nightmare. All I want to do is wake up!"

She draped an arm over her eyes and sobbed. Darkman waited silently, full of a thousand things to say that would never be enough. Only time could heal this wound. But if he could find Shawna, it would take the uncertainty out of this awful situation, speed Julie's recovery. But how? Even the cop named Weatherspoon, doubtless a pro, couldn't do much more than be the bearer of bad news. What could a faceless creature of the night possibly do?

"Is there any way I can help?" he asked when her crying had dwindled to a few hiccuping sniffles. He was holding her hand in his own for the first time in ages, but he could not, through the artificial skin, feel if it was warm or cold, moist or dry. It struck him that his heart might be just as numb. In exchange for control over his distorted rage he was forced to control all other emotions as well, including love. It was not a fair trade-off.

She looked at him. Tiny tears glistened between her eyelashes, gems of grief. She looked both lovely and helpless on her bed of crisp white sheets, but when he searched the deepest portions of his heart as he looked at her he found only memories of fire and pain, loneliness and despair. Beneath his artificial face resided only the charred remnant of the man named Peyton Westlake, who had died and come back to life altered forever, inside and out.

"I don't know what you can do," she said. "I don't really understand why I asked you to come." She gripped his hand tighter, yet he could scarcely feel the pressure. "I didn't mean it like that, Peyton. I know that you wanted to stay hidden until the skin was perfected, and I think I understand. It's just that now, with all this happening, I need people. I can't get through this alone."

Darkman twitched his shoulders. "It looks like Martin will always be there for you."

"He's very nice," she said immediately. "But we're hardly more than friends. I've only known him a few weeks."

He smiled for her, the remains of his facial muscles pulling the skin into something he hoped looked natural. "Your charms work fast, Jules."

"Jules," she said, and smiled a little. "It's been so long since I've heard you call me that. So many years."

"It's only been two years," he told her.

"Seems more like ten."

He looked again at his watch. No big rush yet. "Do you want me to talk to this Weatherspoon guy? He may be holding things back from you."

"I really doubt that, Peyt. The guy's a regular sadist when it comes to telling me the details. He told me exactly how Jerry and Margie were killed, that her throat was cut from ear to ear, that Jerry was gutted."

Darkman's breath left his lungs in a wheeze. "God. Sounds like a swell guy."

"Tell me about it."

He looked at his watch again—an annoying new habit. "Did they still live in the house up north? That subdivision?"

She nodded.

"I think I'll go snoop around there, see what I can find."

"Sure, if you want. But I think the police already did that. And they probably have the house cordoned off."

He shrugged again. "I don't know how else to help you."

"Aw, Peyton," she said, and stroked his hand. "Just being back in my life is help enough. If they ever let me out of this hospital—and they were supposed to discharge me an hour ago—will you come by my apartment some evening? There's so much we could talk about."

"Sure," he said, but doubted it. She would never understand that he had not only been changed by being so terribly burned and disfigured, but that he was not the same man inside and could never be. And what if he lost his temper in front of her? What if a mosquito bit him and he punched holes in her walls trying to kill it? What if he cracked his shin on her coffee table and chucked the sucker out the window in a fit of rage? What she did not need right now was a mental case tagging along behind her. If he truly loved her, he would leave her alone. Perhaps someday she would realize that the greatest act of kindness he could ever do for her was to stay out of her life. Forever.

If he could. Creature of the night or not, loneliness still hurt, even to an insensate soul like his own.

He stood up. It was good to be with her again, but the thoughts it was provoking were distressing. He could do her no good at all.

"Are you going?" she said, surprised. "You just got here!"

He touched his face. "Ninety-nine minutes, remember? You know how vile this skin smells when it disintegrates. The staff would think you were burning tires in here."

She made a wry face. "Point well taken. Could you leave me a number, someplace I can reach you?"

He had to shake his head. "I'm illegally patched into a phone line. If I've got a number, nobody's bothered to tell me what it is."

"Give me your address, then, so I can write you a letter."

"Mailmen don't go to my part of town anymore, Julie. You'd have better luck taping a note on the back of a wino's shirt. I'd eventually see it."

"Then will you call me?"

He nodded this time. "Very soon."

"Tonight?"

"Tonight."

The door suddenly breezed open and a nurse marched in. "I need to check your vitals one last time before you're discharged," she announced, ignoring Darkman entirely. She was wearing a belt of sorts upon which hung several interesting medical gadgets. She disconnected a blood-pressure sleeve and fiddled with it.

"See you," Darkman said, glad for the interruption.

"Sure," Julie said, and waved. "Call me!"

"Will do," he said. "Good-bye, Jules."

He went out. In the hallway he slumped against the wall and regarded the ceiling, breathing through his mouth, his mind reeling with things he should have said. But maybe, he decided, the most worthwhile thing he had managed to say to her was good-bye.

CHAPTER

7

The Ceremony

Osgood Flynn's fear was well founded on that black night as the faithful—a bunch of elderly kooks, by Flynn's own estimation—wearing brown monks' robes filed into the guest cottage. He saw surprise on their shadowed faces. Obviously they had expected to find someone else—say, a teenage girl—strapped to the steel table. He had read in the newspapers that the kidnapped girls had been repeatedly raped. Flynn did not consider himself to be a participant in that perverted ritual; he was simply doing the job he had been hired to do, just as he would have mowed the gigantic lawn if he'd been hired to do so. Besides, he often thought, worse things could have happened to those girls. They could have been held for ransom, forced into prostitution, murdered, and left in the woods for the crows to eat. All he did was bring them here and take them back when the ritual was over.

The last of the faithful came in, some of them carrying smoking sticks of incense. They all stood there gaping at Flynn. He bared his teeth at them, spit sideways onto the floor, flipped them the bird with one captive hand. Silly old coots, he thought. And the first guy who tried to jerk his pants down would get killed when this was over.

The flock suddenly parted as Norman Hopewell strode in wearing a scarlet robe, looking absentminded and distracted under his hood. Fritz trailed in behind him and stood in a corner.

Hopewell walked to the table and turned his back to Flynn to address the crowd. "My beloved," he shouted, and spread his arms as if to embrace them. "Tonight we have a special treat, for God has directed me to set aside one night each year for the Ceremony of Youthful Sacrifice!"

A murmur of wonder spread.

The word "sacrifice" buzzed inside Flynn's head like a bug in a jar. Sacrifice? As in human sacrifice? No way. He struggled helplessly against the straps, then began to shout: "You crazy old bastards ain't getting a piece of me!"

Hopewell turned. "Pipe down, dammit," he whispered fiercely.

"Let me up, you lunatic!" Flynn roared.

Fritz scurried forward, jerked a handkerchief out of a pocket under his robe, and jammed it into Flynn's mouth.

"The holy cloth of silence," Hopewell announced gravely, and turned back to his flock while Flynn thrashed and squirmed, his shouts no more than piglike grunts now.

"My people," Hopewell went on, "in this magical and blessed month of the sacrifice, we can take special pride in our nearness to God. As his newly chosen people, as the immortals, we must offer our thanks. Praise be."

"Praise be," the worshipers mumbled in unison. The stench of sandalwood incense was getting thick. Flynn coughed into the handkerchief, which did not taste particularly clean, and blinked sweat out of his eyes. The room was getting warm and stuffy with so many people packed shoulder to shoulder in the house. He wondered how long this ordeal would last, and if they would really sacrifice him. Nah, he decided. It was all just a ceremony, like taking communion, where they said you drank the blood of Christ and ate his body. It was gruesome-sounding but harmless—just wine and unsalted crackers. Besides, nobody here seemed to be armed. Except Fritz, who was standing now at the head of the table with his arms folded over his chest like a freaking sergeant-at-arms.

And Norman Hopewell was now wondering if the old fools would believe his new routine. They believed that the defiling of a virgin would add years to their lives. They believed that Hopewell was in constant contact with God. They also believed in psychics and faith healers and mediums who spoke to the dead. If Hopewell told them the world was going to end tomorrow they would probably believe that, too. If he told them he had flown here in a UFO piloted by little green men they would probably buy it. But this was going to be a sacrifice, a *murder*, if he went ahead with Fritz's mad plan. What if one of the worshipers, sickened, went to the police?

Yet they had defiled six virgins so far. There were severe penalties for child rape. If one worshiper snitched, the entire group would wind up in jail. Perhaps that would keep them quiet about this latest atrocity, this Ceremony of Youthful Sacrifice—a name that had simply popped into his head from his inborn gift of gab. The faithful paid an exorbitant admission fee every month to participate in the defilement and to hear Hopewell preach. Would they be satisfied with this?

Possibly, he decided. But only if they saw a very, very good show. And that meant that Flynn would have to die slowly on this night. Extremely slowly. And as the capper, perhaps they could eat him—a communion with a real body and real blood.

Well, no, that might be carrying things a little *too* far.

He raised his arms, flapped them like wings. "My beloved," he bellowed, "listen to my words."

For the next hour they listened. Hopewell's diatribe

rose and ebbed and rose some more, building strength, heading for the inevitable thundering climax. In his search for inspiration he had listened to old recordings of the speeches of Adolf Hitler, learned to mimic his frenzied style, watched movies of him to get the facial expressions and gestures right. Norman Hopewell might be a washed-up TV preacher, but he was not without talent. And as the hour droned on, he could see on the wrinkled, spellbound faces of the faithful that, yes, they were believing this, and, no, not one of them would go to the police.

As Edgar P. Fritz stood watching the crowd while the scented candles beside the operating table—the altar—burned away, he was feeling quite satisfied. Hopewell was putting on a fine performance tonight. His speech did not make much sense, but it sounded inspired, even poetic. The man was no genius, but, Lord, could he make speeches! There were times when even Fritz started getting fired up from the force of Hopewell's eloquence, even though he knew the sermon was pure nonsense that was no more divinely inspired than David Koresh's insane ministry in Waco had been. Hopewell was offering his own brand of lunacy. A god of youth indeed. What these old idiots needed was a one-way ticket to a nursing home where they could pretend to be growing younger in privacy while they gummed their pablum.

Fritz was keeping one eye on the straps that held Flynn to the table. The young fellow was still struggling to free himself, sweating and groaning. His efforts would end soon enough, when Hopewell was done shouting and waving his arms. And Fritz knew what the grand finale would be. He knew and Hopewell did not, because Fritz had hidden a long butcher knife inside one sleeve of his robe. If he had given Hopewell the knife before his speech, the preacher would have refused to accept it, aghast. But now Hopewell was giving spirit not only to the faithful but to himself as well. At the apex of his ranting he would suddenly find a knife in his hand. What he would do with it then was simple to predict.

Hopewell rambled on—high, low, high; loud, soft, loud. Sweat poured down his face in streams. The faithful began to clap and shout. From what bottomless well of imagination he dredged up these words Fritz did not know. He only knew that Hopewell was good and that the sermon worked.

Finally he seemed to be at the verge of finishing, bellowing stridently about staying young forever and cleansing their souls with the blood of youth—the youth in question being, of course, the unfortunate Flynn. Fritz had no sympathy for the victim at all. He was a low-life kidnapper and a murderer. The world would be a kinder place when he was dead.

Hopewell was flailing his hands over his head. Fritz stepped behind him and drew the knife out of his sleeve. He pressed it into Hopewell's hand and closed his fingers around it.

"He must *die!*" Hopewell shouted. He spun around, his face distorted with joy and fanaticism, his eyes large and wild. Fritz stepped back, unnerved. Hopewell was in a trance, an insane state. He wrapped both hands around the knife and held it overhead, his thumbs almost touching the ceiling.

"So be it," he hissed. Then he swung his arms downward in a long arc and plunged the blade into Flynn's stomach so hard that the tip clanged against the table.

The crowd went instantly silent. Flynn screamed into the handkerchief, his cheeks billowing in and out. Shockingly red blood pooled around the knife and stained his shirt, seeped out of it and ran across the table in tiny, slow-moving trails.

Hopewell's eyes darted over to Fritz. They were bright with the sudden realization of what he had done in his fervor. He released his grip on the knife and staggered backward.

Alarmed, Fritz began to shout. "For life! For eternal life! Everyone must thrust the holy knife into the youth!"

As a speechmaker he was pretty poor. The faithful looked appalled and fearful. Hopewell shook his head rapidly, blinked a few times. Then a new realization spread across his face. "My beloved, converge on the youth, whom we sacrifice in the name of immortality. We offer this sacrifice as a group, and all of us must thrust the holy knife into his flesh."

The faithful came forward. Almost timidly they clustered around the table. One hardy soul pulled the knife out of Flynn's stomach to the tune of a disgusting slurp, raised it with both gnarled old hands, and buried it in Flynn's stomach again. He stepped back, and other hands reached out. The knife went up, it went down. Flynn shrieked and bucked. Fritz watched, relieved, wishing that at least one of the old fools would stab him through the heart to silence him, but following Hopewell's lead they continued to hack at his midsection. On the floor blood dripped and ran, becoming a dark, spreading stain against the lighter red of the carpet.

Fritz waded through the crowd and found Hopewell leaning against a wall, panting. Hopewell looked wearily at him. "You son of a bitch," he croaked. *"I* wasn't supposed to stab him—*they* were."

"They *are* stabbing him," Fritz responded. "You did fine, better than I expected."

Hopewell's eyes were dull with fatigue. "You set me up."

"Better that than no show at all, Norm. Much better than no show. You did great."

"Save your congratulations for the guy who throws the switch on the electric chair when they fry me."

"That won't happen," Fritz said. "No one will ever get caught."

Hopewell emitted a lifeless, miserable chuckle. "Forty-two people witnessed this ceremony, Fritz. Any one of them could go to the cops."

"Bullshit." Fritz pressed him into a corner, looking around for prying ears. "There's one thing you haven't figured out yet," he said. "After tonight, none of the faithful will dare say a word. None of them."

Hopewell sighed. "Says who?"

"Says me. Look at what they're doing, Norm. Every one of them is helping to kill Flynn. Even the ones who can't stomach it, the old ladies and the cowards, will keep their mouths shut, because they're *accessories* to a murder. If this cult is exposed, all of them will go to prison, and all of them will be hated and scorned by everyone, even their own grandkids."

Hopewell nodded, still looking glum.

"And one other thing you've forgotten: These people believe in you. They believe what you tell them. They believe you talk to God. They believe you can make them live for hundreds of years. Remember how old you're supposed to be? Do you recall what you told them?"

Hopewell almost smiled. "I'm a hundred and sixty-three years old."

"Yeah. And they believe that, Norm, they really believe it. They are so scared of old age and of dying that they will do anything you ask, if they think it will make them live longer. And who knows? Maybe the ceremonies really work."

Hopewell coughed into his hand. "But what happens when one of them keels over from a stroke or a heart attack?"

"Simple. In this group, only the skeptics can die. If one old man drops dead, you tell the rest that he didn't believe hard enough, that he doubted you and your powers. And there's one other thing you probably haven't thought about that will keep these morons in line."

Hopewell thought for a moment. "What is it?"

Fritz smiled. "They love you, Brother Hopewell. The faithful will never turn on the one they love most. You are completely safe."

Now the preacher brightened considerably. "By God, Fritz, I think you're right." He turned and took a few steps, then raised his arms. "My children!" he shouted.

The old people stopped and looked at him.

"To the holy mansion when you are done, where we must sing and dance and prove that we are getting younger every moment! Does everyone here feel young?"

They all cheered, even the old lady who was slowly driving the butcher knife into Flynn's stomach by holding it steady with one hand while pounding on the handle with the other.

Flynn was motionless now, either unconscious or dead.

"Follow me!" Hopewell shouted. Then, quietly to Fritz: "I trust you'll clean up this mess."

"Don't I always?" Fritz replied, and watched Hopewell and his crazy followers file out to party the rest of the night away.

CHAPTER

8

The Phone Man

Darkman's face was gone by the time he was close to home, but by then he was in the deserted core of the city where the population consisted only of rats in the buildings and winos in the gutters. A weight seemed to lift from his heart as he approached the soap factory. This was where he belonged, not just where fate had deposited him. He needed solitude, a place to think.

Or a place to go mad?

He almost groaned. His internal tormentor, his alter ego, was coming back to life. He wondered if he really possessed two personalities, if he was already insane. After all, he had once been a scientist and was now a freak. Why not talk to himself? When he was unmasked, sure as hell no one else would talk to him.

He had left the soap factory chained shut with a bicycle chain and lock he'd found some weeks ago. It had been a simple task to program one of his computers to generate a random series of likely numbers, but it had taken several hundred tries before he'd found the right combination. A way, at least, to fill his days with more than just experiment after failed experiment on the skin.

Sometimes he wanted to trash all of the equipment, give up forever, and hire himself out to a carnival sideshow as the Amazing Burned Man or the Stupendous Skull Face or the Fantastic Fried Fellow. Perhaps have a fling with the Bearded Lady, eat dinner with a sword swallower, milk the two-headed cow once in a while.

No doubt about it, Darkie old chum, you have cracked.

He opened the lock and hauled open the soap factory's huge front door. The smell as he went inside and pulled the door shut was the smell of home—dust, rat turds, pizza and Kentucky Fried Chicken boxes rotting in a corner. Kicking his way through discarded Coke and beer cans, he entered the huge main chamber of the factory where all of his scientific equipment was arrayed on tables suspended from the ceiling. He stopped and folded his arms over his chest, thinking about Julie and their short encounter. He had in many ways expected more, uh, *concern* from her. After all, she knew he was a walking advertisement for mercy killing, that he was holed up here in the bowels of the city's sleaziest area, that he was lonely. But what had he found? Julie holding hands with some flashy rich boy. She had treated Darkman like an old friend and nothing more.

Isn't that the way you wanted it? he asked himself.

Well, yes. He had vowed to stay out of her life until the skin was permanent. But he had never thought about her finding another man. It would be a tragedy if he came back to her forever but had to compete with someone for her love. He was not good at that sort of thing.

Once as a kid growing up in Indiana, he'd had a crush on a girl in high school named Peggy. Out of the blue some big kid had walked up and told him Peggy was his now, that Peyton's date with her was canceled, that he'd get a fat lip if he so much as looked at her again. Peyton, never the competitive type, had said that was fine with him, even though he liked Peggy a lot. The two later got married, and he'd heard that the boy had become a wife-beater who regularly knocked Peggy into the hospital.

Such was life.

Indeed, he agreed with himself. Peggy had gotten a bitter surprise as she aged. So had Peyton Westlake. And Julie, too. Come to think of it, did he know anyone on this planet who had not somehow discovered that the great master plan of his life had turned out to be the great disaster plan of his life? Sudden tragic diseases, crippling car wrecks, financial catastrophes, early death. Did anyone ever truly escape the harsh realities of life in those unpredictable years between twenty-five and forty, from young adulthood to that scary midlife crisis? He doubted it. Even a tycoon like Martin Clayborne probably had a sob story or two to tell.

Which meant, maybe, that being burned alive wasn't the worst thing that could happen. It happened all the time.

But most burned people didn't get their brains messily rearranged by the Rangeveritz procedure. Most burned people didn't wind up insane. And insanity, quite possibly, was the very worst thing that could happen to anyone. With a leak or two in the old brain bucket it was hard to function, hard to enjoy life. Some people, he supposed, probably thought of insanity as a carefree time bouncing around in a rubber room. In reality, he knew with a good degree of certainty that being crazy meant living in abject misery.

He was walking to his shredded old office chair when an idea hit him, and hit him hard. He was not a cop or a detective, he was not a caped crusader, but he did have money, a whole briefcase full of it, and what better way to investigate a murder-kidnapping than by enlisting a lot of other people in the search? A lot of other people as in the population of the entire city, every single person?

No. It was silly, a dumb idea. It wouldn't work.

But what if it did?

He knew what he had to do now. He went to his telephone and snatched up the receiver, pressed it to the remaining flap of his right ear, and dialed Information for the number of Midwestern Bell.

It was time to get a telephone number like everybody else.

He barely had time to disconnect his illegal patch-in before the gray and yellow van stopped out front and a portly little man in uniform climbed out. Darkman had to admire him for his promptness. He had expected to wait all day. Since it was too late to make a new batch of skin—the process took the better part of twenty minutes —he wound some fresh gauze around his head and hands to keep the hapless telephone man from having a coronary if he saw him. It was never much good for the old ego when people screamed or fainted at the sight of his butchered face.

The Midwestern Bell man, wearing a walkie-talkie on his tool belt, ambled up and pecked on the door, looking as if he doubted anyone lived in this junk pile. Darkman saw him look around uneasily, reach into a back pocket, and produce a small silver flask. It winked under the sun as he tipped it back. Then presto, it was gone. The man dabbed his lips with his sleeve.

Darkman, wearing sunglasses over his bandages, pulled the door fully open and stepped into the light. A pair of highly suspicious eyes took in the sight of him. "Yo, gramps," the man grunted. "Nasty sunburn?"

"I need a phone number," Darkman said.

"Don't we all. Plastic surgery?"

"I already have a phone. I just need a hookup."

"Bad acne?"

"And a number. The phone is rotary, not touch-tone."

"Psoriasis? The heartbreak thereof? Scabies? Shingles?"

Darkman sighed. "I got burned in a fire."

"I knew it." He stepped back outside and looked up, shielding his eyes with one hand. "I didn't even know we still had lines working here. Have you had a phone before?"

"Yes."

"Then I guess you'll have one again." He went to the pole, which stood to one side of the building looking lonesome. It was one of the old-fashioned ones with prongs sticking out to form steps. He rubbed his hands and started up while his walkie-talkie came alive and spit out something crackly and unintelligible. Darkman frowned. What a career for a drinking man.

He went back inside and parked himself in the rusty bones of his chair. Lying on the keyboard of the computer in front of him was a wrinkled sheet of paper he'd been writing on. It was blurry with erasures. He picked it up with his thickly wrapped hands, took his sunglasses off, and read it for the fiftieth time. An author he was not, but it was the best he could come up with. He crossed the huge dirty room, and located the briefcase propped against a wall. Seated in the chair again with the case on his knees, he thumbed the latches and lifted the lid.

Fifty thousand bucks, give or take. He could not do better than the police when it came to finding Shawna and the men who had murdered her parents. But he *could* enlist a lot of people to help him. At first the idea had seemed pretty lame, but the more he'd thought about it, the more sense it had made. He latched the briefcase shut and reread the sheet of paper.

Footsteps interrupted him. The phone man wandered in carrying a large city phone directory, his head jerking around as he took in the dark and dismal factory. "Yo, gotcha hooked up," he said. "Creepy place," he added. "Whatcha do here?"

"Secret government project," Darkman said. "Very hush-hush."

"Wow."

Darkman located a pencil. "Got my new number?"

The phone man was turning in a circle. "Nah. I need to call the main office. Computers and all that. Are you FBI?"

"More secret than that."

"CIA?"

"No. Interpol."

"I knew it. Uh, what's Interpol?"

"International Criminal Police Organization."

"Cops?"

"Secret agents."

"Aha. Here, let me test the phone." He put the phone book down, picked up the receiver, and dialed. "This is mobile T-twenty-eight," he said into it. "Fourth and McKenzie, repeat hookup. Got a number for this unit yet?"

He lowered the receiver. "They're getting it. What's that noise?"

Darkman shrugged. "What noise?"

"Like a motorcycle, kinda."

"Oh. My generator."

"No juice here?"

"No, just a phone line now."

"Damn city's dying, I can tell you that." He took his flask out of his pocket and extended it. "Gin?"

Darkman shook his head.

"I hate heights," the man said, and drank. He made a face, wagged his head, capped the flask. "Heights scare me silly without my medicine." He lifted the phone again. "Yeah, still here. Okay. Yo, gramps!"

Darkman perked up.

"Ready to write?"

He nodded. The man gave him his phone number, then hung up. He made more small talk while Darkman waited for him to leave, kept talking while Darkman escorted him to the door, talked all the way to his van. Finally he drove away, and Darkman, anxious to get on with things, hurried back inside. He sat and pulled the telephone close, found the number of the city's largest newspaper in the directory, and read his note aloud to the advertising department: "Fifty-thousand-dollar reward for information leading to the arrest and conviction of the persons responsible for seven kidnappings in seven months. Anonymity guaranteed. Phone 555-2094."

The ad would fill one whole page and run for three days if he paid for it in advance.

Grumbling, but not surprised, he started to manufacture a new batch of skin so that he could enter the real world once again, hoping that his efforts would not be a waste of time and money.

CHAPTER

9

A Hasty Burial

It was nearing two o'clock when Pocketknife, drowsing behind the wheel of his Caprice as the moon floated overhead, caught sight of Fritz carrying something down the lane. Pocketknife did not know what had become of Flynn, but in this unpleasant line of work he'd learned the value of keeping his mouth shut. He sat up straighter and rubbed his eyes. After the old people were done with their rituals, the girls were usually so hysterical that they had to be kept in the trunk.

He got out and twisted open the wire that held the trunk shut, then waited for Fritz to deposit the ex-virgin inside. But in the wandering light he saw that it was not the girl that he and Flynn had brought earlier. It was Flynn himself. It took an effort of will not to ask Fritz what had happened to him.

Fritz dumped Flynn into the trunk, then straightened with a grunt. "Dispose of his ass," he said gruffly. "He can't be found."

"Okay," Pocketknife said, and let the lid fall shut. He twisted the wire a few times, feeling cold and hollow inside. They had killed Flynn. But why? "I'll get the girl," he said.

"Wait." Fritz put out a hand to block him. "The girl stays here. I'll call you next month for a new pickup."

"Right," Pocketknife said. "Same pay?"

He nodded. "You're a solo act now, kid, so you'll be earning double, like you did tonight. Just make sure you're not being followed, and for Christ's sake, bury him deep."

"Okay."

Fritz turned on his heel and stalked away. Pocketknife saw his portly silhouette in the moonlight stop and lift a limp bundle from the ground. Oh, yeah, the girl. Fritz carried her to the top of the hill and vanished into the dark.

Pocketknife got into his car again, his face slack and disbelieving. It took some time, as usual, to get the Chevy started, but in the end the old engine turned over. He backed up, then shifted into drive and idled down the hillside, trailed by a thin cloud of dust. Shortly after the first turn he stopped with a brief squeal of the brakes. He pushed the emergency brake and got out with the car still running. Curiosity and dread were eating at his mind.

He unwired the trunk and lifted the lid. Moonlight cascaded in.

"Jesus," he uttered. A chill slid down his spine. He bent low, examining Flynn, squinting in the poor light.

"Man," he whispered, "why did they chop you up so bad?"

He dragged Flynn out, too spooked to drive the corpse any farther. Panting, he dropped the body into the ditch beside the road and hurriedly threw a few handfuls of dirt and last year's leaves over him. "Okay, Mr. Fritz," he mumbled. "Flynn is dead and buried."

He wired the trunk shut, noticing that it smelled bad—an animal odor, like raw, bloody meat. He almost gagged on it. He got back inside the car and lit a cigarette to chase the memory of that smell away. His skin was crawling, and he began to see weird shapes among the moon shadows of the trees. It was with relief that he slammed the door. He cranked the window down a bit and flicked ashes through it.

Something made a noise as he put the cigarette back to his lips. Something groaned in the darkness where Flynn's body lay. Pocketknife's eyes grew as large as a pair of eggs. Without further hesitation he pressed the accelerator to the floor and peeled out, the emergency brake forgotten, his Marlboro dangling from his lips and eventually dropping unnoticed onto his lap. It wasn't until he smelled burning cloth that he let out a curse and beat the cigarette to death with his fist.

Norman Hopewell was drunk out of his mind when Fritz brought the girl in through a back door and locked her in a closet. Over the pounding music of the Sex Pistols, even over the roaring conversation of the old folks as they danced and panted to the beat, Fritz expected to hear Hopewell whooping it up, could imagine him prancing around in his socks and red robe with a bottle of booze in either hand. There were times when Fritz believed, as he did right now, that without his services to the grand guru the whole scam would fall apart.

Instead he found Hopewell collapsed on one of the sofas in the gigantic living room, only one hand clutching a bottle, apparently having passed out. The pungent aroma of sweat and incense was warm and thick. Fritz nudged him.

Hopewell sat up and saw two Fritzes, both of them looking disgruntled. He blinked, and his vision swam back into focus. He wondered what time it was, where he was. His last memory was of doing the Watusi with a naked woman whose dentures fell out halfway through the song. Oh, yeah, the mansion, the cult, the whole brilliant scheme. To his eyes the room was pitching and rocking, to his ears the music was loud enough to wake the dead. "Whaddya want?" he asked.

"I stashed the girl in a closet," Fritz shouted in his face. "Where do you want her?"

"Girl?" Hopewell scratched at his dark hair, frowning. "I don't remem . . . Oh, her! Take her up to my bedroom." He smacked his lips; his tongue felt woolly and thick in the pasty wasteland of his mouth. How much of that damned brandy had he drunk tonight? Two bottles? More? It was very hard to think. The room was littered with empty bottles and cigarette butts. Some of the faithful had shed their clothes in the heat and tossed them aside. Several were snoozing on the floor. It was one hell of a party, no doubt about it. And in the morning the old fools would be bent and stiff and sore, but they would swear they felt ten years younger.

He stood up, swaying and bleary-eyed. Looking down, he saw that someone had barfed on the floor. Perhaps he had done it himself. "My bedroom," he said again. "Tape her mouth shut and tie her to the bed. I'll be up when this shindig is over."

"Good enough," Fritz said sourly.

"Did you clean up the mess in the guest cottage?"

"Everything's as it was," Fritz said. "We need to replace the carpet anyway, and the only thing that really got ruined was the knife."

"Did you get rid of it?"

"Gone forever."

"Good." Hopewell smiled. "A month's vacation will feel good, huh? I don't know about the faithful, but my back is killing me."

Fritz walked away, bumping into old people, shoving them aside. Hopewell, realizing that he still had a bottle in his hand, drank some more brandy. It burned like liquid fire and for a terrible moment he thought it might come back up, but then the sensation was gone and he began to feel better. The virgin was in his room; her only task in life now was to give him pleasure. Imagine that. He knew that she would need time to adjust to the situation, that at first she would cry and scream as she had outside, but in the drunken wreckage of his mind he could see her eventually falling in love with him, marrying him when she was of age. He believed that after a woman—even a very young woman—was introduced to the pleasures of the flesh, she needed to be serviced almost daily in order to satisfy her needs. He had been married briefly at the age of twenty, and he was sure he knew just about all there was to know about women. His hapless bride was unfortunately dead now, gunned down by a stranger in her home while Hopewell was away. Such a terrible thing.

He'd paid a man fifteen thousand dollars to kill his wife. That contract had marked the start of a lasting partnership between the two. The man's name was Edgar P. Fritz.

A woman who looked like the wicked witch of just about any direction sidled close and jabbed Hopewell with an elbow. He smiled at her and began to dance, not because he wanted to—ten hours of sleep sounded better—but because she was a paying customer, and that was what, in the end, it all boiled down to.

Money. For Norman Hopewell, there was no finer thing in the world.

Dawn came, and the thirty-four men and eight women members of the Church of Eternal Youth and Beauty eventually wandered out to their cars and drove away, staggering with exhaustion, coughing, moaning. Hopewell would not see them for a month, which would give them time to recuperate. In a few days, feeling much better, they would convince themselves that by partying like teenagers they were becoming younger. In a way, Hopewell assumed, he was indeed helping them to live longer. After all, exercise never hurt anybody, and what better way to shock an ailing old liver back to life than by bludgeoning it with alcohol?

Hopewell was already asleep in his huge water bed when the sun began its climb into the morning sky and the last of the faithful drove away. Fed up with the noise and the party, he had been unable to last the whole night and had sneaked upstairs at about three. Now a few shafts of sunlight were stabbing through his bedroom windows. He awoke with a monster of a headache threatening to crack his skull open like an egg. He groaned and shifted, trying to remember who he was and where he was. He had long ago decided that he would make a lousy alcoholic. Even the drunkest of the drunks knew their own name when they woke up.

He forced his watering eyes open and saw a white ceiling and a small crystal chandelier. The blue velvet curtains were open, allowing painful light inside. Then he did remember in a tumble of memories that took shape and became believable.

The mansion. The sacrifice. The party.

His fine new career.

The virgin.

He sat up with a groan, hearing his spine crackle and pop, and looked around the room with eyes that were stitched with bright threads of red.

She was awake. Fritz had tied her to a bookcase beside the head of the bed with strips of cloth torn from a sheet. Her ankles were spread and tied to the bedpost. Her pajama top—he saw now that it had little white lambs jumping little brown fences on it—was devoid of buttons and lay open. For a moment he was stunned: she looked so young! In the moonlight she had seemed older. But she was beautiful, despite her puffy eyes and sweaty hair. In a few years he would make her his bride.

He looked at the ornate silver clock on the wall: six-thirty. Outside a lawn mower was blatting and rattling. Perhaps that was what woke him up. He made a mental note to have Fritz fire the groundskeeper; the fool should know better than to cut grass at the crack of dawn on a Saturday. After the Friday night ceremonies, Hopewell required lots of sleep.

He kept looking at the girl, blinking sleep out of his eyes. She watched him with her pale blue eyes full of fatigue and fear. It came back to him now that she had been squirming and writhing when he fell into bed. A few hard punches had ended that in a hurry, but now her face was bruised. His perfect bride was damaged.

"My poor darling," he whispered, and leaned down to kiss her. She snapped her head around, and he got a faceful of hair and dead grass.

"You little twit," he snarled, and slapped her.

She began to squirm again, screaming through the green washcloth Fritz had stuffed into her mouth in lieu of tape. Her shriek was muffled, but still it made his head ache harder. He crawled out of bed, woozy and disoriented, and stood there barefoot, naked, and sick, but still just drunk enough to find all of this a little funny. He wandered to his dresser and looked at himself in the mirror, almost giggling. He looked like a walking corpse.

Somebody rapped on the door.

"We don't want any," Hopewell wearily answered.

The door popped open. It was Fritz, not looking very good himself. "We got a problem," he said.

Hopewell noticed two things immediately: one, Fritz looked green and scared, and two, he had a rolled-up newspaper in one hand. Neither item disturbed Hopewell much.

"I'm not even dressed yet," he spat at Fritz. "Close the frigging door."

He stepped inside instead.

Hopewell found a robe and slipped into it, then turned back to his partner, impatient and upset. "Okay, you've delivered the morning paper like a good little boy," he said. "Leave us alone now."

Fritz strode up to him, batting his knee with the paper. "Cut the bullshit, Norm." He glanced at the girl.

Hopewell thought he saw fear in Fritz's muddy brown eyes again. How odd.

"Okay," Hopewell said. "What's wrong?"

Fritz unrolled the newspaper and pulled out a single page. "Look at this. Special insert, printed so recently it still smells like wet ink. Take a good look at it, Norm. Then you'll know what's wrong."

Hopewell took it. The print was huge, taking up the whole page: "Fifty-thousand-dollar reward . . ."

"Jesus Christ," Hopewell muttered. "Does that mean us?"

"You bet it means us."

"Who in the world has fifty grand to throw around like this? What's the connection?"

Fritz grabbed the paper back. "What you see is what you get, Norm. We're finished. The church will have to be disbanded. We've got to run and run fast. Most people would sell their right arm for fifty thousand bucks, and we've got forty-two followers to worry about, not to mention that little chicken Pocketknife. Especially Pocketknife."

Hopewell frowned. "You hired his ass. I didn't," he said. "And my faithful won't turn me in. Just like you told me last night, they love me. They think I'm God's right-hand man."

Fritz tossed the page aside, grabbed the lapels of Hopewell's satin robe, and jerked him back and forth. "Wake up and smell the coffee, Norm! Last night I let you have your fun with the girl, but this is a new day, a new and dangerous one! We—me *and* you—have to get out of town as fast as we can get!"

Hopewell pushed him away. "I refuse to abandon my flock. I have a duty to my beloved."

Fritz gaped at him as if he had become a large and possibly poisonous insect. "You're nuts," he said wonderingly. "Do you actually believe all this shit you preach about the gods and eternal youth and all the rest of it?"

"I believe God has ordained that I should meet my future bride at a tender age."

Fritz took a backward step, his face drawn up with incredulity. "She's a little kid, Norm. She's been kidnapped and tied up and raped. That moron Flynn killed her parents. And you expect her to *marry* you?"

He sniffed. "In time she'll discover my charm."

"Good God." Fritz rubbed his face where a stubble of

whiskers had started to sprout. "Look. I'm going to town to buy two plane tickets to Rio. We've got enough money to last us for a while. Maybe we could even start this cult of youth crap down there, sucker the rich tourists. But we have got to *run*, Norm—now, this morning. That phone number in the paper is probably being dialed right now."

"I wonder who ran that ad," Hopewell said. "The FBI?"

Fritz snorted. "The FBI doesn't hand out rewards like that. One of the girls we bagged must have a rich uncle or something, and you can bet he's pissed. He'll probably hike the reward up to half a million bucks over the next few days . . . so we can't wait that long. I'm packing and getting out of here within the next ten minutes, with or without you. Which will it be?"

Hopewell looked at the girl. Her naked chest already bore hints of the things yet to come, things men would practically die for. He could not let them have her. "I'm staying," he announced. "Staying with my bride. Send me a postcard from Rio now and then."

Fritz attached an ugly lopsided sneer to his face. "You've flipped," he said stonily. "I always knew you were on the edge, but this time you've wigged out for good. Consider me gone."

"Good-bye. *Hasta la vista.* Write when you get work."

"Goddamn fruitcake," Fritz muttered, and left, slamming the door hard enough to rattle the wall.

Hopewell eyed the door for a moment, then shuffled around and leered at the girl.

"My precious bride," he murmured and dropped to his knees beside her. "I will make you a very happy woman. You'll see."

Slowly, reverently, he began to kiss her bare feet, fondling her insteps and the strips of cloth that bound her ankles. When she moaned, his heart leaped; already her love was budding. He was working his way closer to her knees when his head jerked up suddenly. He frowned, his eyes flicking back and forth. He wagged his head to clear it.

A fifty-thousand-dollar reward! He would turn in his own mother for that kind of money were he not already getting rich. Most of the faithful were rich, but hey, if you got a million, all you want is another million. And that stupid jerk Pocketknife—what would *he* do for that much money?

He pushed himself onto his feet, his eyes bright with sudden realization, and ran to the door, almost tripping over the hem of his robe.

"Fritz!" he shouted as he wrenched it open. "In the name of God, wait a second!"

CHAPTER

10

Phone Fun

The first call came at 6:35 A.M., jangling Darkman out of
sleep. He rolled off the rectangle of fiberglass insulation
that was his bed and darted across the room to the
telephone, his heart picking up speed as he made his way
past the scattered heaps of trash. It had to be someone
about the ad and the reward. No one else knew his
number. Then again, it could be some company interested in shampooing his carpets, or MCI wanting to
know if he was fed up with AT&T yet, or any one of a
hundred other nuisance calls. Maybe even a heavy
breather getting his early-morning kicks.

He snatched the phone up on the third ring and
pressed the receiver to his ear. To say hello, or something
more official? "Hot line," he heard himself say. Not bad
at all.

"I'm calling about the kidnappings." It was a man.
Judging by the wheezing and the cracking voice,
Darkman put his age at around seventy. The background
noise suggested that he was calling from a busy place,
perhaps a nursing home or hospital. Possibly he was
related to the kidnapper, perhaps even the kidnapper's

very own father, abused and afraid, living in terror of his criminal son.

"You have the right number," Darkman said with reassuring professionalism.

"I know who took them girls," the old man said. "I been telling people what I know, but they get afraid and they won't help me."

"I'm here to help," Darkman said.

"They been kidnapping them at night, and it's been going on longer than seven months, I'll have you know. Ever since we licked 'em, they been using our foreign aid, getting stronger, taking the world one chunk at a time."

Darkman frowned. "Pardon me?"

"The goddamn Japs. I fought the slanty-eyed little bastards on Guadalcanal, and I been fighting 'em ever since. You ain't gonna see me in no goddamn imported car! I buy American! And the Krauts! Goddamn Nazis, still trying to take over the world! Know what I call them damn Volkswagen cars? Nazi wheelbarrows! The Japs sell us them goddamn rice rockets, and Hitler's still tooling around in a Mercedes-Benz down in Paraguay! We licked 'em once and we'll do it again!"

Darkman pulled the phone away from his ear and looked at it while the man ranted loud enough to shake the receiver. So much for his detective instincts. The guy was a nut. He put the phone back in its cradle gently, cutting the guy off in mid-sentence. Well, with a big ad in the morning edition he should expect some cranks to phone in. Come to think of it, some people might call with bogus information, hoping to claim the reward. Well, the ad said "leading to the arrest and conviction" before any reward was paid, and it said nothing about a consolation prize for originality.

He had headed for the bathroom, where one of the ancient showers still could spit water, when the phone rang again, a shrill cry in the cool, gloomy dawn. He turned and jogged back, picked it up. "Hot line."

It was a woman this time. "Do I have the party I've dialed?" she asked. "In re the kidnappings?"

In re? "You do," he said.

"The kidnapper has to be my ex-husband," she said. Her voice was low and stiff, as if her nose was in the air and her neck was heavy with jewels and fur. She sounded rich, but her accent sounded phony. Darkman blinked. One crank call, and already he was making judgments based on the sound of a voice. Maybe this woman had valid information. Perhaps her ex-husband was predisposed toward kidnapping and sexual molestation.

"Tell me more," he said in a very businesslike tone.

"Reginald," she said, "is an absolute cad. I'm familiar with these kidnappings and the crimes perpetrated upon those poor girls. You see, Reginald and I have been divorced for two years now, two dreadful years made bearable by the simple fact that I do not have to look at his face across the breakfast table by the pool anymore. You see, I caught Reginald—actually, it was a detective I employed who caught him—having a simply *torrid* affair with a woman young enough to be his daughter, some twenty-year-old *tramp* he met God knows where. Why he would risk his marriage and his good standing in the community for the sleazy backyard wiles of a *child* I shall never fathom. I'm quite willing to forgo any reward, but I did think that you police should know that Reginald has a nasty, *nasty* record of carousing with young females. I—"

"Ma'am?" Darkman interjected. "Does, uh, Reginald have a police record?"

"I should say so!" she blurted. "Speeding tickets to the tune of twelve hundred dollars! The man—and I use the term grudgingly—has regressed to the age of about thirteen and can now be found *daily* at the little slut's house or tearing around the city in a sports car at high speed. And do you think he *married* the little tramp? Not my Reginald. No, marriage is for old fuddy-duddies like, perhaps, his long-suffering *ex*-wife. Why, not one week ago he . . ."

Darkman was staring at the phone again. He put the receiver down, not quite as gently as before. Who did the old bag think he was? Dear Abby?

Ring!

He grabbed it up. "Hot line."

"Does that mean fifty dollars or five hundred, like Barry says?" A kid, by the sound of the voice.

"Neither," Darkman said. "It's fifty thousand."

"'Kay. Bye."

Darkman hung up, disheartened. Even little kids were getting into the act now.

It rang again. "Hot line."

"Yeah, police?"

"Sort of," Darkman said, hoping this guy wasn't a nut. Maybe this call, finally, was from someone with useful information.

"If some guy's camping trailer is parked in his carport, but a good eighteen inches is sticking out over my property line, can I make him move it?"

Darkman shrugged. "I don't know."

"Fat lot of help you guys are."

Click.

He looked at the phone. He put the receiver down.

Ring!

"Hot line."

He listened. His jaw dropped a little. "Flying saucers?" he said. "There's no life on Venus." He listened some more. "Kidnapping humans for what? Breeding? Life can't survive there. The surface temperature is over nine hundred degrees."

Pause. "Mars either. Thin atmosphere. Listen, you really—"

Click!

He hung up. The ad was certainly an attention grabber, if nothing else. He knew that the newspaper's circulation was about thirty thousand, but had not known that every nut in the city was a subscriber.

Ring!

"Hot line. Uh-huh. Uh-huh."

It was some guy.

"Sure, I've read the Bible. No, the money's just a reward for information."

He listened, then hung up. There was a bad taste growing in his mouth now, and he had to use the bathroom soon.

Ring!

"What?"

Seconds passing.

"Listen, why don't you just take a flying leap? And don't call back."

Ring!

"Hot line!"

Time passing.

"There's been no suggestion of cannibalism. You do? Drop dead!"

Ring!

And so the morning went.

Norman Hopewell caught up with Fritz on the upper floor of the mansion. He stood breathlessly watching Fritz unload his dresser drawers into three large suitcases. The bright morning sun cast squares of light on the carpet and Fritz's rapidly moving feet.

"We don't have to run," Hopewell panted.

"Get real, Norm," Fritz said nastily. "The jig is up, to borrow a phrase." He snapped one suitcase shut and shoved it aside. "The whole scam's about to backfire, and I don't want to be within a thousand miles of here when it does." He began hauling socks out of drawers in a frenzy.

"It won't," Hopewell said. "I'm not letting a year's worth of work fizzle out like this, a year of working my way to the top, sacrificing chickens and dogs and cats to get the faithful prepped for the virgin thing and the human sacrifice thing. I've invented the perfect religion for the rich and the decadent. Do you really think I'll go back to shoveling burgers?"

"What you shovel here is crap," Fritz snapped. "What's the difference?"

"Funny. Do you really expect me to take my act to Rio?"

"They'll be taking you to prison if you don't."

"Wrong. You've forgotten how the faithful adore me. They think I possess divine powers."

"Yeah?" Fritz stopped and put his fists on his hips. "The only power you'll be getting is a couple thousand volts in the electric chair, big shot. Can't you feel it starting to sizzle already?"

"Christ, man, knock it off. I really do have a plan, a good one. Careful planning, that's what I've always been good at. This religious garbage was my idea, my plan, and it worked. Now I have a better one."

Fritz laughed. "Oh, really? Right about now one of the flock is dialing the phone to make himself richer, unless Pocketknife beats him to the punch. There's no more time for your hokey plans."

"We can take care of Pocketknife," Hopewell said. "And the faithful are sleeping it off right now, every single one of them. They won't even be reading the newspaper until this evening."

Fritz eyed him, looking just the slightest bit interested now. "All right, Norm, lay it on me. And then we leave."

"We'll just see about that. Edgar, partner of mine, how long would it take us to get ahold of some guns? Say, about forty-four of them? One for you, one for me, one for each person in the flock."

"What?"

"Guns. You know, barrels and bullets and all that. Bang-bang."

"I know what a goddamn gun is, Norm, but what do we need guns for? This plan sucks already."

"Be patient. Our harmless cult—almost harmless—can become a team of armed fighters."

Fritz rolled his eyes. "Forty-two old farts carrying guns around like a SWAT team? If I wasn't so scared I'd laugh. And then I'd throw you out a window."

"Bear with me." Hopewell squared his shoulders. "The secret of the cult's success is and always has been our unity. We are a group of people with a common goal: eternal life, and I don't mean flapping around in heaven like a giant bug. I mean physical life forever."

Fritz went back to his packing. "I think I've heard this before."

"What would you give to live forever? What would anybody give?"

"An arm and a leg," Fritz replied dourly. "Next stupid question?"

"Thus we have a common goal, my people and I. And even you. When our flock reads the paper we will grow even stronger. They will fear getting caught at this as much as you do, and no one will spill the proverbial beans."

Fritz folded a pair of slacks and put them into the suitcase. Hopewell took his silence as a sign that he was willing to listen to the rest, so he went on, warming to the topic. "What great statesman said, 'If we do not hang together, we will surely hang separately'? Patrick Henry? Makes no difference. You see, the faithful have participated in a lot of weird ceremonies, often revolting ones, and they've loved every minute of them, paid a lot of money for the privilege."

"So what does that have to do with guns?"

"Just this: some clown wants to buy information so bad he's advertising it in the paper. We have to make that information expensive for him, very expensive. We have to *unite*, my good partner, and with that unity we can overcome the power of that reward money."

Fritz stopped packing. He swiped at a line of sweat that was tracking down his forehead. "Makes good PR, Norm, but no sense. What in the hell are you trying to say?"

"Simply put, we inform the flock that anyone who squeals gets shot. They can put some of us in jail, but they can't put all of us there. If even one of us blabs to the cops, the rest will have orders to kill him. There can never be a trial because there will never be a witness. We'll take an oath, swear to the god of youth that we stand united against the forces of evil, that the cult will never be exposed. We'll hold an emergency meeting tonight and hand out guns. I'll make a speech."

Fritz shrugged. "Now I'm really scared. You're starting to make sense."

"Of course I am. Who among us would dare call that phone number with over forty guns aimed at his head? Would you?"

He ignored the question. "So where do we get forty-four guns?"

Hopewell shrugged. "I make the speeches; you handle the details. There are sporting goods shops left and right downtown. Just take some cash and get some real flashy stuff, machine guns and all that."

Fritz shook his head. "Machine guns can't be bought without a special license, and pistols have to be registered. I think I can get a bunch of rifles, though."

"Fine, guns are guns."

Fritz had a shirt in his hands; he stuck it back in the drawer. "You know, I really ought to have my head examined for even considering this." He pushed the remaining empty suitcase under the bed. "Your plan leaves out one important detail, though: Pocketknife."

"Ah." Hopewell smiled. "That is another matter I'll leave for you. I might suggest buying his silence with money. I might further suggest hiring someone to kill him."

Fritz stroked his chin with his pudgy fingers. "Could be arranged, I guess."

"Good. I'll get on the phone, start spreading the word. We'll have a Ceremony of Youthful Unity and cap it with a Ceremony of Youthful Defilement. Then we'll pass out the guns."

Fritz frowned. "Where are we going to get a girl for the defilement ceremony on such short notice?"

Hopewell pointed toward his bedroom. "We've got one already."

"Her? I thought she was your bride."

"One defilement won't alter that. Besides, I think she'll enjoy it. You know how women are."

Fritz's expression made it clear that he did not know at all. He picked up the two suitcases, put them on the bed, and began to unpack. "I wouldn't have liked Rio anyway," he said. "Too far away from civilization."

"Exactly." Hopewell turned to leave. "I've got things to do. It's going to be a long day, but I know just how to start it out right."

He went out. A minute later Fritz heard the girl begin to grunt and squeal, heard a few slaps. He shook his head with dismay. Norman Hopewell was one very strange fellow, but Fritz had to admit that his plan seemed workable. World leaders had taken similar actions a hundred times, inventing an enemy and fomenting a war in order to unite their disgruntled followers and stave off revolution. And it had worked every time.

He finished unpacking and left the room to find a phone book and let his fingers do a little walking through the Yellow Pages under "Guns and Hunting Supplies."

Some lucky dealer was about to make a huge sale.

CHAPTER

11

The Mystery

Julie was watching a talk show on TV when she heard a tapping on the door of her apartment. She stood and trudged away from the couch, wincing from the pain caused by her skin grafts whenever she walked. She knew that in her fuzzy black bathrobe she looked like a penguin, but did not care much. Besides, it was probably just her neighbor across the hall, Mrs. Elkhart, wanting to see if she was okay. Then again it could be the police, here to give her more tragic news. She unhooked the chain and opened the door a crack.

Martin Clayborne stood there smiling, dressed to kill. He was holding the morning paper, unopened and still wrapped with a rubber band. She let him in.

"Good morning to you," he said happily. "How's the old body burn treating you?"

"Still hurts," she said, returning his smile. "Could I interest you in some coffee? I might even have a doughnut or two."

"Sounds great, but you just sit back down and heal. How does breakfast in bed sound?"

"I'm already up. See? The TV's on."

"Breakfast on the couch, then. What are they blowing off about this time? Reformed lesbians in love with their grandfather's uncle?"

"Close," she said. "Former nuns turned prostitutes."

Martin laughed and tossed the paper on the couch. God, but does he look good, Julie thought. Rich and handsome and a really nice man. What more could she want? She lowered herself onto the couch with a grimace while he strode into the kitchen. He banged things around for a while, humming to himself. Julie used the remote to search the other channels, but found only new cartoons that couldn't hold a candle to her favorite, Bugs Bunny, and shut the set off. The day would come, she hoped, when talk shows would run out of bizarre topics and quit. The world would be a better place.

Martin's voice floated out of the kitchen. "Julie, how do you like your eggs?"

"Over hard," she replied. "None of that runny stuff."

"One steamroller special, coming up. Toast?"

"Sure."

"What?" He poked his head around the corner.

"I said yes. Toast."

"Okay. Bacon?"

"Sure." He nodded, vanished. She heard the toaster go down, began to smell coffee. Martin was too good to be true. He could dine with the mayor, hobnob with senators all day, probably even visit movie stars. Instead he chose to be with her, cook for her. A few weeks ago she would have sworn that no man like him could ever exist, the perfect catch. Best of all—and the thing that scared her—was that he was spending thousands to open up her own law office, for no more reason than the fact that he liked her. She knew she was not hard to look at, knew that her figure was good, but stacked up against a movie queen she was Plain Jane for sure. And so far he had not once tried to do anything more than kiss her briefly.

Oh, and she just remembered, he had even given her a car. "Say, Martin?" she said.

His head appeared. "Yes?"

"I just now remembered that my car is still parked outside my new office building. Do you think they've towed it away by now?"

"Fear not," he said with a grin. "I had it brought here while you were in the hospital. Got it washed and waxed, too."

"Amazing," she said. "One of these days I'm going to wake up from this dream and find out you don't really exist."

He simply laughed and went away again. Something was sizzling in a skillet now—bacon, by the smell of it. She picked up the paper, slid the rubber band off. The headlines were mostly about an economic summit someplace in Europe, your average boring stuff. She opened it and found a huge ad instead of page three. Curious, she glanced over it.

Good grief. She read it again, feeling happy and confused and intensely curious. Of course Martin Clayborne had placed it. Who else could afford to run a full-page ad and offer a huge reward? Only him. Unless the cops were offering that kind of money, and that didn't seem possible.

"Hey, Martin," she said loudly, competing with the noises of his culinary efforts.

He ambled out of the kitchen wiping his hands with a paper towel. "Yes, Julie?"

"That's an awful lot of money."

"Indeed?" He raised his eyebrows. "Do I get three guesses what this might be about?"

"You know. The ad in the paper."

"Oh, that." He walked over and sat down beside her. She showed him the page. "Must've cost you a thousand dollars."

He frowned. "Actually, it's a good idea, but I didn't place it. Honest."

"Really?" She read it again. "Who would be willing to spend that kind of money?"

He twitched his shoulders. "Maybe one of the kid-

89

napped girls comes from a family with money. Fifty grand isn't all that much when you've got a million or two."

"It's enough to get the worms to crawl out of the woodwork. I think it's a great idea."

"No word on Shawna yet?"

"No. I'm beginning to think her kidnapping isn't related to the other ones. First of all, her parents were murdered, and that doesn't fit the modus op. Second, she hasn't been released yet—also not the typical M.O."

"Any word about a ransom demand?"

"*Nada*. It's as if she dropped off the face of the earth."

He disengaged the paper from her hands and put it on the coffee table. "Listen," he said quietly. "You might have to get used to the idea that Shawna won't be coming back. If your brother and his wife were murdered, why would the guy take it easy on her?"

"No," she said. "I refuse to dwell on that. Tina was unharmed. It's possible that the murderer broke in to steal things, got jumped by Jerry and killed him, then killed Margie to keep her quiet. But he didn't have the nerve to kill a thirteen-year-old girl, and Tina probably slept through it all."

"Which leaves Shawna a hostage."

"Yes. But he didn't kill her, see. He didn't then and he won't now. My guess is that to keep her quiet he'll have to keep her with him. And that means that eventually she'll find a way to escape."

Martin spread his hands. "Possibly. If it makes you feel better, hang on to that idea, and I won't spoil it for you. In any case, Shawna might be gone a long, long time."

"I think I'm bearing up well. Mom flies in this afternoon, and I've handed the whole matter of services and burial to a funeral home. Jerry wasn't a big believer in life insurance, but he did have a thirty-thousand-dollar veteran's policy. It'll pay the expenses and leave Shawna and Tina a decent sum. Plus, if I can sell the house, there's another ninety thousand or so."

He scowled. "Houses where people have been murdered are hard to sell. Have you listed it yet?"

She attempted a smile. "I called Clayborne Realty. One of your people is handling it now."

"We won't take a commission," he said immediately. "Shawna and Tina will get every cent."

"That's good of you, Martin."

"How are your finances doing?" he asked. "You've been off the job for a long time. I can loan you some cash, if you want."

"Thanks, but no. I do have a little bit saved up."

"Just so you're not going hungry."

"Not to worry." She sniffed suddenly. "Speaking of hungry, I don't really like incinerated bacon."

"Whoops!" He jumped up and charged into the kitchen, and she heard him scraping and banging. Julie let herself fall back against the cushions, wondering about the ad, the reward. Who could have done it? Probably the father of one of the kidnapped girls, just as Martin said. Either that or Peyton, who had mentioned something about having a little money, but no, fifty thousand dollars was far beyond his means now. To her knowledge he didn't even have a job. But then, how could he, looking the way he did?

For a moment she felt a strong urge to weep. Her world had been turned upside down when Peyton vanished, and it got turned upside down again every time he returned. And now this tragedy, this uncertainty. She only hoped she could hang on to her sanity long enough to see it all through. Her only consolation was that Tina was safe and would soon be living in Connecticut with her grandmother Hastings. It had occurred to Julie to take her into her own home, but as a lawyer she was in and out constantly and often had to work late. Alone here was no place for a little girl recently orphaned.

But back to that curious offer of a reward. All she had to do was dial that number and ask what the scoop was. Besides, she was closely related to one of the victims and had a right to know.

She got the phone and dialed 555-2094. It was snapped up before the first ring was finished. "Pertinent calls only," someone blared in her ear. "The reward will be given only for valid information. All crank calls will be referred to the police, and the callers will be prosecuted. Okay, what have you got to say?"

She hung up guiltily, feeling bad for having wasted someone's time. It was like dialing 911 and asking a silly question like "How's the traffic downtown" or "How much does it cost to get a license renewed?" Well, so much for that.

Martin came back with her breakfast on a lap tray covered with a dish towel. He unfolded the little wire legs and set the tray down gently. *"Voilà,"* he said, and whipped the towel away. Smoke drifted up in a thin gray cloud. He offered her a napkin. "Burned bacon, soggy toast, rubber eggs, rancid orange juice, and turpentine-flavored coffee. What would madam like for lunch?"

"A new cook," she muttered with good humor, and tried to eat the stuff.

CHAPTER

12

The Power of Hate

Osgood Flynn, stabbed over thirty times in the stomach, was finding death hard to come by.

Since coming to his senses—sort of—and realizing that he was in deep, deep trouble, he had been able to drag himself forward a few inches at a time. Around him a scene of desolation and dense woods was lighted by a bloated moon. He had no idea where he was or how he had gotten there, only that he was in ferocious pain and was lying in a small puddle of blood with dead leaves stuck to his face and to his arms, with their decoupage of tattoos.

The memory began to come back to him, scraps of recollection, shards of awareness: Hopewell and his crazy followers, the knife, a sea of people hacking at him again and again. Flynn could think of no reason why he was still alive. When he felt his stomach, along with fresh pain came the realization that his life was leaking out of too many wounds to count, all of them spaced within a small area. Perhaps, he thought, they were all doctors and knew where to stab a man without killing him fast. With that thought came the terror that they had simply been toying with him for ghastly reasons of their own and that they might come back to finish him off.

Lying in the moonlight he found that by using his elbows he could scoot slowly forward. He wanted badly to look behind him, see how far he had traveled in the endless night, but any movement of his torso caused the pain to rocket to the top of his skull like a small bomb exploding inside him. And yet he felt nothing in his legs at all. He did not have to go to medical school to figure out what must have happened: his spinal cord had been severed, probably in that first horrifying moment when Hopewell stabbed him with all his insane strength. Flynn could remember hearing the screech of metal against metal, could remember stupidly thinking that Hopewell had bent the damn knife. Then the pain had sprung alive and he could do no more than shriek and strain.

He felt cold now. Too cold. A balmy morning was settling into these woods, and yet he was beginning to shiver—a bad sign. He was slipping into shock and certain death. His mind was jittering out of control, becoming hazy. He wanted very badly to sleep, but to sleep would be to die. Instead he licked the dirt off his lips and kept crawling.

When his consciousness gelled again a bit later, he found himself in dense woods having to detour around huge trees, utterly lost. He wanted to believe that there were houses nearby, but he did not know where he was. If Hopewell and that fat little bastard Fritz had dumped him off, he could very well be a hundred miles from civilization—in another state, even, though he did not believe that. Any man who'd been stabbed so often would be presumed dead, no questions asked. In his fevered mind, now full of the noise of his own teeth chattering, he considered it highly likely that they had simply pushed him out of a car not far from the mansion, which meant that if he crawled far enough, he would find help.

His head dropped suddenly down as his strength failed, his ruined stomach stitched with pain and spasms, aware that he was becoming nauseated by the stench of his own blood and was too tired to move without a rest. He told himself as he lay panting that he was Osgood Flynn, that he was mean and tough and young, that he would die of old age on some murky day in the future, but not on this day. He had too much left to do. Besides, he had killed people, and not just the husband and wife at the virgin's house, not just two or three others. By his own count he had murdered eight people during his career as a hired killer. With each murder had come new strength, new power. He was not very familiar with Indian legends, but he did believe that by killing others he could capture their stamina, their life-force. What else could explain his ability to survive the multiple stabbings?

So he would live, and he would drag himself to safety. He would live to heal, live to get revenge on Hopewell and Fritz and every other fool who had dared to try to kill him, a completely innocent stranger. Even if he spent the rest of his life in a wheelchair, dead from the waist down, he would have his revenge.

He almost grinned, imagining the way he would make them suffer and die. And that bastard Pocketknife, who had sat still and quiet as he, Osgood Flynn, was dragged off to be killed, he would pay. All of them would pay. But for now the only thing he could do was crawl and rest, go and stop, bleed and hate.

He dragged himself forward again, freezing even as the day grew hotter, leaving a trail of mashed leaves and blood behind his unfeeling, bobbling feet.

CHAPTER

13

The Morning Blahs

Later that morning Pocketknife was rolling over in bed while nightmares flashed through his brain. He saw girls' faces twisted with fear, a man and his wife slashed and gutted and bleeding, Fritz carrying a body to the car like a sack of grain and dumping it into the trunk, handfuls of dirt and leaves tossed over the mangled body of a man named Flynn. Evil things done in the night.

Something thumped in another room, and Pocketknife's eyes jerked open, bloodshot eyes narrowed to slits against the morning sunlight flooding through his bedroom window. He turned over again and crushed his face into his pillow. His head throbbed, a dull jackhammer between his tortured eyes. The nightmares were real; waking up had done nothing to erase them. But screw it and screw them. In his pants pocket was an envelope stuffed full of money, and that was all that mattered. This time it was double payment. Stupid know-it-all Flynn. Hopewell and Fritz had probably murdered him for killing those two people in that nice suburban house. Why Flynn had found it necessary to do that, Pocketknife would never know.

Smells filtered through the crack under his bedroom door: bacon frying in rancid grease, the cheap perfume his mother sloshed on herself before she went out whoring. Oh, no, wait. Not whoring. She had boyfriends. *Boyfriends.* Every night she left this tenement apartment full of kids and went out with her *boyfriends.* That was why she had so many kids, none with the same father. That was why she lived in a tenement.

The smells were making him sick. Behind his eyelids he could see the whole scene: his mother in her frayed bathrobe, her hair a matted brown tangle, her fingernails painted a flaking barn red like her lipstick, makeup smeared around the bags under her eyes, a cigarette drooping from her lips as she made breakfast for the kids. So damn many kids. Pocketknife had nine brothers and sisters, two of them coffee brown, the color of Dottie Hursch's former boyfriends.

Crockery clinked and banged. Silverware rattled in a drawer. Now eggs were beginning to sizzle. The sound ate into Pocketknife's brain, chasing the sleep he'd missed and now needed. Kids were clumping around in the other rooms, getting ready for another fun day in the slums. The neighborhood was springing to life after a dead and dreary night in the tenements.

Pocketknife jerked himself to a sitting position. *"Quiet down!"* he screamed.

The racket continued. Pocketknife stared at the flaking paint on the wall like a man contemplating his own tombstone. His room wasn't a bedroom at all, just a nook in this decaying building that happened to be big enough to fit a bed into. He had moved in here to get away from all the kids and have a room of his own. It hadn't done any good. There was never any sleep to be had after sunup.

"Little bastards," he muttered, and swung himself slowly out of bed. His head throbbed from the overdose of Flynn's vodka. The open bottle, almost empty, was still on the floor where Pocketknife had left it. He kicked it aside and watched it hit the baseboard, then rebound and spin, spewing the last drops. It didn't matter; he could afford to buy more vodka, a lot more, but the smell of it made him sick. He stood up and fumbled in his pocket for a smoke. The pack of Marlboros was empty. He crushed it wearily into a ball and tossed it aside, then yanked his door open and went into the kitchen.

His mother glanced at him, looking just as he had pictured her. The ash on her cigarette was almost two inches long, the smoke curling up past her bulbous nose and wreathing itself around her messy hair.

"What's wrong with you?" she grunted.

"Out of smokes," he grunted back, looking with sick and weary eyes at the battered kitchen table with its load of cracked plates and bent silverware. There had been a day, not seven months ago, when he had sworn to himself he would use his kidnapping money to get himself out of this place, but the money seemed to disappear like cigarettes, up in smoke. He had three thousand dollars in his pocket now. What had happened to the fifteen hundred he'd earned last month? A month of bottles and girls and white powder up the nose, and *poof*, it was gone. And he was still here.

"Sit down," Dottie said.

The thought of breakfast made his stomach squirm like a beached eel. "I ain't hungry," he said.

"So don't eat, then."

He spied her pack of Salems on the countertop and shook one out. When it was going good he leaned back and inhaled deeply of it, hating the menthol taste, worrying vaguely about his lungs.

"You look terrible," Dottie Hursch said, working at the stove. The ash fell off her cigarette into the skillet. She stirred it in.

"I met a nice man last night," she said, grinning with secret mirth as she turned the eggs in the skillet. "He said I was pretty as a picture."

Pocketknife snorted. Mom and her fantasies. Meet the right man someday, get married, move out of this hellhole forever. She was on her last legs, and she knew it. At forty-two she was so far over the hill that a new hill loomed up ahead, one she would never cross.

"So who's the dreamboat this time?" Pocketknife said sourly. "Tom Selleck?"

"I can't recall his name exactly. Robert or Rupert or something. I'll meet him again."

In hell, Pocketknife thought, but did not say it.

She paused in her cooking to take a long drink out of a bottle of Calvert's gin, which she kept beside the refrigerator. She made a face and licked her lips, then stuck her cigarette back into her mouth. "He took me to Denny's for a late supper."

"Which Denny's?"

"The one by the mall on Eastridge. I told you he was nice."

"Big deal," he said.

"Kids!" Dottie Hursch yelled without warning. "Breakfast!"

Pocketknife winced. After two hours' sleep on a bottle of cheap vodka, his head swelled and ebbed, steady as a tide. His eardrums rattled as small feet thundered over the wooden floors, eighteen feet in worn-out shoes. The kids charged in, chattering, fighting, generally whooping it up as they sat down at the table. The oldest of them was fourteen. That had always been a mystery to Pocketknife. He was twenty. Why had his mother waited another eight years to have kid number two? Had she discovered that she would get extra welfare checks? Had she discovered a new and exciting way of making money, sort of like part-time work, peddling the products of her uterus like Avon or Tupperware? The thought of it revolted him.

"Settle down!" his mother screamed, holding the hot skillet over their heads. They quieted down and leaned back in their chairs. Eggs and bacon were dutifully doled out. Dottie Hursch went to the cupboard and opened it to reveal row upon row of colorful boxes of Pop-Tarts.

She was a Pop-Tarts freak, Pocketknife had discovered at about age nine. So were the rest of the brats. Pop-Tarts gagged Pocketknife. Many things gagged Pocketknife.

All of the kids got Pop-Tarts. Pocketknife smoked his borrowed cigarette and thought of the money in his pocket as he watched the brat pack eat. Double bucks for easy work. The hardest task had been burying Flynn, the big talker, with his stomach sliced up.

Well, kind of burying him.

Pocketknife shuddered. It had been spooky there in the dark, but nobody else used that overgrown lane, so there was no need to worry about the body being found. Flynn would rot in peace. But still, the memory of the burial gagged him.

He noticed his mother looking at him curiously. She was leaning against the stove, her bathrobe parted obscenely above her knees, her furry slippers looking like freshly killed Easter Bunnies. She dropped her cigarette in the sink, still watching him while it fizzled there.

"Did you find a job or something?" she asked finally.

He jerked. "Huh?"

"The booze. The snort. You've been living it up like a billionaire Hughes. Did the Laundromat take you back?"

"No."

"What, then?"

"I got a different job, if you have to know."

"Good for you, deadbeat son of mine. Where?"

"A place."

"Doing what?"

Pocketknife breathed a little harder. He puffed on his cigarette, hating its menthol. "Driving," he said at last. "I drive."

"What? A truck?"

"Yeah."

"How much do they pay you?"

Pocketknife looked at his feet. There was something about his mother's eyes, something in them he had never been able to lie to very well. Maybe it was the pain he could see there, the same kind of pain he could see in his own eyes when he looked hard into a mirror.

"Minimum wage," he mumbled.

"That's better than nothing," she said. "Can you spare a few bucks for your mom?"

He looked back up at her. "What for?"

"A little something for the cookie jar. You might remember that you're a little too old to be living at home for free."

No welfare check for a grown kid, in other words, Pocketknife thought, but as usual kept it to himself. He was deadwood around here and knew it quite well.

She held out her hand. "A buck or two, Percy. If you're working, you can pay room and board. Don't you agree?"

"Don't call me Percy," he muttered sullenly. And Flynn thought *his* name was stupid. Pocketknife dug out the envelope and extracted two twenties from the bundle inside. The rest went back in his pocket.

"Hey!" one of his brothers screeched. "I saw that! He's got a ton of money!"

Pocketknife turned on him, snarling. "Shut your face and eat your Pop-Tart."

"A ton of money?" Dottie said. "What, yesterday was payday?"

Pocketknife stared at her. "Yeah, it was payday."

She eyed him. "How much is a ton?"

"Two thousand pounds!" one of the little girls blurted out. She looked around proudly with egg yolk drooling down her chin. Her name was Joan—no middle name, just Joan. Dottie had gotten weary of naming kids. "I make straight A's in school," Joan said, smirking. "A ton is two thousand pounds. Ha-ha."

"Show me," Dottie said.

Pocketknife held the two twenties out. "Take them."

"Let me see the envelope."

Pocketknife stuck his cigarette in his mouth and put his hands and the twenties protectively in his pockets. "Ain't nothing to see."

"A ton of money!" the brother with the dark skin shouted. "Two thousand pounds of money!" He turned and sneered at his sister. "I get A's too."

"No you don't!"

"Bet I do!"

"*Kids!*" Dottie pointed a finger at Pocketknife's face. "How much is a ton of money, Percy? A hundred dollars? Two hundred?"

Pocketknife stared at her. The smell of bacon was thick and sickening in the hot morning air.

"You've been freeloading for years, Percy, and I haven't said a word. But if you're making money by the ton, you're gonna share it. Your brothers and sisters need shoes. We need food, clothes, lunch boxes for the kids. Now show me!"

Pocketknife pushed himself away from the counter and went into his room. He spit his cigarette on the floor and kicked the door shut, ignoring the giggles, the chuckles, the whispers. He fell face down on the bed, his hands still in his pockets, making the rusty bedsprings creak. He felt like a corpse, stiff and useless, just like Flynn under his burden of dirt and leaves. What was the sense of it all?

The door wafted open.

"If you're doing something that makes you a ton of money, then you're doing something illegal," Dottie Hursch said, "and I won't have my kids be illegal. We may be on welfare, but we've still got our pride. Now show me how much money you've got."

"Go to hell," Pocketknife said into his pillow. It smelled of sweat and dried spit, and it gagged him like everything else. Why couldn't she leave him alone?

"Show me."

He pulled the envelope and the two twenties out of his pocket and dropped them on the floor.

Aware of her bending down beside the bed, he clenched his teeth so tight they hurt. In the darkness of his pillow he saw Flynn's body in the trunk of the Caprice.

"Jesus," he heard her whisper.

She straightened. Money crackled through her fingers. "How did you earn all this?" she demanded.

"Working."

"Where?"

"I drive for a rich dude."

"Swear it."

He raised his head, turning it to look at her. All he could see was her bathrobe and slippers, the dead Easter Bunnies. "I swear it," he said.

"Are you selling drugs?"

"No."

She dropped the envelope on his back. "Just be able to live with yourself, Percy. For money like this, you can sell your soul."

He rose up suddenly, spinning over to a sitting position. Then he was on his feet. "So?" he screamed. "You sell your body! You sold yourself last night for a free meal!"

The slap, when it came, was not hard enough, would never be hard enough to hurt the monster that had taken control of Pocketknife's soul.

She left, slamming the door.

He bent and retrieved the envelope.

"You're no better than I am," he whispered as he stuck the money back in his pocket.

But the monster coming to life inside him insisted it was not so.

CHAPTER

14

A Clever Disguise

By noon Darkman was ready to act. All morning long he had hovered around the phone like a buzzard circling carrion. When it rang, it was almost always some con artist on the scent of a fast buck. At least the nut cases were interesting; the liars would go so far as to say they'd seen a kidnapped girl working at a carnival or slinging burgers at some faraway place, unaware that all of the girls except Shawna had been returned. More than one disgruntled wife had called to sic the law on her wayward husband.

So far he'd had only two calls that seemed legitimate, one of them very much so. It had come from a man who claimed to have seen a red-haired girl being pushed out of a blue Dodge van while he was driving to work early one morning last month. She looked to be about fourteen, seemed to be a heavy-metal punk type in jeans and earrings and chains. Darkman did not know if any of the kidnapped girls had red hair, but he jotted down the man's number.

The second promising caller was a young girl named Joanna Wyles. She said she was a friend of one of the girls who had been kidnapped four months ago and who was currently under psychiatric care. After being released by the kidnapper the girl had wandered to Joanna's house, let herself in, and stumbled upstairs to Joanna's bedroom muttering something about "them." She was a rumpled mess, but her hair had been braided into two long ropes by someone who was very good at it; the girl had never worn braids before in her life. As if in a trance, she had shed her shoes and started blowing on her bare feet. The skin between her toes was severely burned and covered with a substance that flaked off like wax.

Did the cops know about that? Darkman wanted to know. Yes, Joanna told him. But she knew something else, something she had not told anyone for fear of adding even more horror to an already horrible story, a part of the story that the abused girl, she felt sure, would never remember. In exchange for this information Darkman had to swear never to repeat it.

He swore. Joanna hemmed and hawed in the embarrassed and pained way only an adolescent could hem and haw. He could sense that she was cupping her hands around the phone for privacy. And then she whispered the secret to him.

"Jesus," he whispered back. "And the cops don't know this?"

Joanna said she could not bring herself to say it in person to anyone, not even to her own mother.

Darkman took her number down and thanked her.

When he hung up, Darkman was shaking with outrage. The girl in question had been eleven years old.

"Them," she had said. There had been more than one kidnapper, then. Two, ten, twenty? There were some very sick people in this town. No dungeon was deep enough to chain them in, no hell hot enough for their perverted souls.

Joanna, unaware of the need to preserve any evidence, had talked the girl into taking a shower. She said it was like talking to a dummy. In the bathroom Joanna had helped her out of her clothes, and . . . and . . .

Something had fallen to the floor and rolled. Joanna had danced away, screaming into her hands while the other girl stared stupidly at the walls. It was a floppy length of pink rubber, an artificial penis that Joanna had called a "fake weenie" because she did not know such a thing was commonly called a dildo. But it . . . had fallen . . .

It had fallen . . . out of the girl.

Darkman walked to the Bio-Press and flipped the switch that turned it on, his stomach heavy as cold steel. Moving quickly, he turned the rest of his equipment on. Machinery clicked and buzzed, warming up.

Time to become somebody. Time to do something besides hover around the phone while Shawna Hastings was similarly tortured.

It was time to become Darkman in earnest.

Darkman arrived at the Hastings family's suburban house, the scene of the murders, at about one-thirty. The afternoon was sunny and hot, the air cleaner and fresher there than in the guts of the city. He got out of the cab, paid the fare with a ten-dollar bill, and stood with his hands on his hips, surveying the scene. He remembered that he had once been here with Julie. Shortly before they became engaged, she had taken him to meet her relatives so they could pass judgment on him. The visit had gone well; Peyton Westlake had passed the test.

The house, a light blue aluminum-sided affair, had been cordoned off with yellow tape that announced to the neighborhood that no one could cross except the police. There was no one around; the investigators' work was likely finished by now, and the evidence was being studied in a lab.

Darkman was now a candidate for look-alike champion of the week. Working from memory, he had programmed the computers and the Bio-Press to create a likeness of the chief of police, Jackson Goodrow. His photograph was often in the newspapers, and he sometimes appeared on television; Darkman had even met him face-to-face once at a college fund-raiser. Physically their dimensions were about the same—tallish, slim enough, no slouching. Best of all, Goodrow rarely was seen in uniform, preferring the currently popular businessman image.

Feeling secure, Darkman ducked under the tape and stalked past some hedges to the front door. The jamb was split and broken; he pushed the door open and nearly walked into a cop standing there.

"Good afternoon, Officer," Darkman said, temporarily unable to see much in the relative dark.

"This is a restricted area," the cop snapped. "Do you . . ."

Darkman smiled at his sudden loss for words.

"Chief Goodrow," the officer said, flustered. "Sorry, sir."

"It's all right," Darkman said, trying to imitate Goodrow's well-known genial gruffness. "I decided to take a look at the scene myself, get a better feel for this case. The mayor is eager for some progress."

"Yes, sir. It's a very difficult case, sir."

"Maintain your post. And keep everyone else outside. I'll need to concentrate, and the last thing I need is the press barking at my heels."

The cop nodded. "Yes sir," he said avidly. "Will do."

"Good." Darkman walked deeper into the house wondering, and not for the first time, just what he hoped to find here. He was not a detective, and he certainly wasn't a psychic investigator, but he believed that no matter how hard the police had tried, they might have missed something. It was not his goal to aid their investigation; if he found something useful, he would use it himself. The kidnappers had no right to waste the people's tax money on a drawn-out trial or, worse, to get themselves off the hook via a technicality. When Darkman found them, they would know what true justice was.

And was that fair? Was it just?

He almost laughed. How fair and just had it been when Peyton Westlake was tortured and nearly killed? Every single one of those crooks was now dead.

Now, *that* was justice.

The pale gray carpet bore crusted, splattered red stains. Dried blood dotted the area like fat raindrops. It was here, then, that Margaret's throat was cut. He deduced that she had been standing when it happened. Hence the wild spray. Jesus.

The furniture was in its rightful place, just as he remembered it. There was a pink slipper on the floor splashed with blood, framed with tape. A square of tape indicated a place on the coffee table where something had lain, either a large book or a magazine. Blood had splashed near it. There didn't appear to have been much of a struggle. Very likely the murderer had caught Margaret by surprise.

Near the couch there was an odd stain on the rug. It looked like chewed-up macaroni and cheese. Darkman frowned, squatting beside it. "Officer," he said, "did the lab come up with anything from this?"

The cop looked over. "Somebody puked there. Nothing special was found in it, unless you call vodka special."

Darkman rose. To his knowledge Jerry didn't drink, at least not enough to make him vomit all over the floor. One of the kidnappers had thrown up, but why? Was he sickened by the bloodbath or just drunk out of his mind?

In the kitchen there was nothing remarkable. Margie had been a housecleaning maniac, if he recalled correctly, who had given him a fairly dirty look when he propped his feet on the coffee table; she had promptly charged off to get a dustcloth when he finally got the message and removed them. His consolation had been that he was a scientist, and scientists were so smart they were entitled to be slobs. Or something like that.

He went up the carpeted stairway and into a bedroom,

veering around a huge red stain at the head of the stairs where Jerry had died. The room contained an unmade child-size bed, a dresser, pink carpeting, kiddie things tacked to the walls—Tina's room, obviously. He dropped to his hands and knees and looked under the bed, wondering why he was doing it, seeing nothing, not even dust balls. He got up and checked the doorknobs, saw fingerprints that had traces of detection powder on them. Apparently none of them belonged to the perpetrators, or the perpetrators had no prints on file, or the perpetrators were too smart to leave prints.

He checked the next room. Unmade bed, blue carpet, teenage things—Shawna's room. The house was not new, but it sure smelled that way—fresh wallpaper, furniture polish, and new rugs. If Margie had been a clean freak, Jerry had been a workaholic. So much effort, and such a dismal end.

He wondered what was happening to Shawna right now. He had to shove the thought from his mind.

The remaining room—master bedroom—held nothing of interest. The bed was not made, suggesting a late-night crime. The house stood absolutely silent save for the muted buzzing of an electric clock and a gentle hissing from the breeze outside.

So what had Darkman accomplished here?

Nothing that he could think of. He was just seeking a launching pad for his personal investigation. He would start at the scene of the crime, then spread out from there. Hell, even Sherlock Holmes had done it that way. But—and this was a big but—Holmes usually found something the police had missed. Failing that, he saw in the evidence something no one else had thought of. But how did he do it?

He did it this way, Darkman thought unhappily. A guy named Arthur Conan Doyle sat down and wrote a bunch of novels, and in those novels he could make Sherlock Holmes do anything he wanted. In reality, no man had that kind of talent.

But what *would* Holmes do if he were here? Darkman wondered as he went back down the stairs.

So where did that leave Darkman? For one thing, he lived in a factory full of high-tech computer equipment, some of it his own design. But the police had labs, too. He had the freedom to do as he wanted, move as he wanted, investigate things as he wanted. The cops were handicapped by the current laws. They couldn't force a suspect to talk. Darkman could. Oh, you bet your life he could. But . . .

He didn't have any suspects to talk to yet.

He sat on the bottom step and put his elbows on his knees, his chin on his hands. The cop at the door had his back to him and was keeping mercifully quiet. Darkman began to rack his brain. Who was behind this barbarity? Who could possibly benefit? One of the girls had burns and wax between her toes. No one knew that but Darkman and his young informant. That girl had been molested, brutalized in a spectacularly obscene, perverted way. Who would debase a young girl like that, a girl who was still a kid? All of the victims had been painfully young. Which meant they were fresh and untouched. They were . . . *virgins?*

Yes, they were virgins. And the wax and burns between their toes?

Candles?

Virgins. Candles.

It didn't fit. In ancient cultures people had sometimes sacrificed virgins to appease the gods. They were told by their murderers that it was the greatest honor a young girl could receive. The most beautiful virgin in the land was offered to the gods.

Religion. This had to be tied to a religion. But to debase children? To defile virgins? To burn candles between their toes, braid their hair, then humiliate them utterly?

A cult. A religious cult that kidnapped virgins. Why not? There were probably a dozen oddball cults in this state alone. Devil-worshipers, animal sacrificers, guru followers, people who hid in caves waiting for the end of the world, deranged religionists who drained the blood out of cows. Darkman nodded to himself, considering the possibility that a cult consisting of at least two members had kidnapped a virgin once a month, put her through hell all night, then released her. But now, during the seventh month, they had changed their routine: they had sacrificed her.

His heart sank. If this was true, the insanity was reaching new peaks. From now on the kidnapped girls would be killed instead of tortured or, more likely, tortured and then killed.

Which meant Shawna was dead by now. Or suffering an unspeakable agony before being killed.

Where was she? Shackled in a barn or basement, candles burning between her toes? In a dungeon strapped to a rack? Chained in someone's home? There was no way of knowing.

He stood up, dejected, not even caring how much longer his face would last. His hot line had yielded new facts, but he was nowhere near a solution. This house had nothing to offer but mute testimony to a massacre. In this disguise he could gain access to all of the unfortunate girls, interview them, but surely the police had done that again and again.

Which left what? He was certain the kidnappers belonged to a religious cult of some kind. Perhaps the police did not know that. Such a cult would have to be well hidden and quiet, its members sworn to utter secrecy. But how to find it, penetrate it?

His eyes jerked open wider. Darkman could do something even Sherlock Holmes couldn't do. He could disguise himself entirely and completely, not as a cop or a plainclothes police detective or even a private eye. He could disguise himself as something even better and use money as bait.

He could disguise himself as a wealthy man who

wanted to join a group of people who did terrible things to virgin girls in a secret place.

He said a quick good-bye to the cop and left the house, then jogged toward the rim of the subdivision where a main artery led back into town, a street where he could flag down a taxi and set his plan into action.

CHAPTER

15

A Family Matter

Percy Hursch, known to the world as Pocketknife, was half asleep, slipping in and out of dreams, with his pillow lying over his face, when he heard his mother shout: *"Damn!"*

He sat up in bed. His pillow flopped to the floor, covering the vodka bottle. The room, overheated by the sun, smelled like a tavern. It made him feel nauseated.

"Man!" Dottie Hursch hollered from the kitchen.

Groaning, Pocketknife got out of bed. He wobbled on his feet, cursing under his breath, and patted the envelope full of money in his pocket. His eyes felt hot and fevered in their sockets. Even though all the kids were playing outside, it was impossible to get any decent sleep. And his loudmouth mother had no consideration for a man with a hangover.

He went to his door, flung it open, and squinted into the sunlight that flooded through the grimy kitchen windows. "What the hell are you shouting about?" he snarled, folding his arms across his chest.

Still in her pink robe and slippers, she was sitting at the table, which was littered with plates from breakfast, reading the newspaper, a cigarette dangling from her lips. A glance at the battered clock told him it was almost one. So much for sleep.

"Look at this," his mother said, removing a page from the thick local newspaper. "Somebody wants to give away fifty thousand dollars."

"Whoopee," Pocketknife muttered. He patted his shirt pocket and remembered he was out of smokes. He got one of his mother's and lit it. The menthol burned his aching lungs like dull fire. "Is that a good reason to wake me up?"

She looked at him with a hint of a sneer curling her lips. "Shouldn't you be up anyway? You have to drive your truck, remember? Isn't that your new job?"

He ignored the taunt. "So what are you yelling about? You got a job too?"

"No, and I wouldn't need one if I knew something the cops could use." She showed him the page. "If I knew who the kidnapper was, I'd be on easy street."

As Pocketknife read the ad his heart gave a single heavy thump in his chest. His mouth dropped open, and he immediately clicked it shut. He swallowed, trying to remain nonchalant, but a strangled squeak escaped his throat.

Dottie looked at him curiously. "You look sick all of a sudden," she said.

Pocketknife squared his shoulders. Now his heart was beating regularly again, only a little too fast, as if he had just run a short sprint. He puffed on his borrowed cigarette, returning his mother's stare. "Just this hangover," he said, and averted his gaze. Damn her eyes, he thought miserably. She looked as if she knew something, knew everything. But that was impossible.

"I wonder who'll hit the jackpot on this," she said, looking at the ad again. "Fifty thousand dollars." It was a dreamy murmur. "Imagine that."

One of the kids burst into the kitchen, breathing hard, grinning from the simple joy of being young and alive. It was Robbie, Pocketknife recalled with difficulty. Dottie

Hursch was no genius at names. He often wondered why she had saddled him with the name Percy. Maybe just to make sure he'd get beaten up in school every day. It had worked.

"Mom," Robbie said breathlessly, "Joan fell down and scraped her knee."

"So? Is she bleeding to death?"

"No, but she's crying."

"Tell her to keep her crying outside. Percy's got a headache."

"Percy's got a headache," Robbie imitated in a high, girlish voice. "Mr. Hotshot Percy has a headache! Ho-ho-ho!"

"Ho-ho this, brat," Pocketknife snapped, giving him the finger.

"Wow!" Robbie said, coming up behind his mother and ignoring Pocketknife. "How many thousands are those?"

"Fifty," Dottie replied. "Fifty thousand dollars. It's a reward."

"For what?"

She held it closer for him to read. Shocker of the year, Pocketknife thought: the kid could read.

"Let's call them up and fake it!" Robbie blurted when he was done. "We'll tell them we know who did it, and we can collect fifty thousand dollars. Then I can get a new bike!"

"You shut up!" Pocketknife snapped.

"We'll tell them Pocketknife did it," Robbie sneered. "We'll tell them Mr. Hotshot Percy kidnapped seven people for an envelope full of money!"

"You shut the hell up!" Pocketknife shouted. His heart was racing now, and he felt greasy sweat trickle down the back of his neck. The kid was just taunting him—he knew that, of course—but still his heart raced and his neck sweated. The monster inside him squirmed and hissed.

"Percy did it!" Robbie shouted. "Percy did it!"

Pocketknife lunged at him, knocking the table sideways. Plates wobbled off the edge and shattered on the floor in a series of crashes.

Robbie jumped to safety, sneering, smirking, ready to bolt. "Percy did it!" he cried. "Ho-ho-ho!"

"Little bastard!" Pocketknife heaved the table fully aside and stalked toward him, reaching out with his arms.

Dottie stood up and blocked his way. "Leave him alone!" she shouted. "He's just making fun."

"I don't like his kind of fun." He aimed a threatening finger at his brother. "You'll be sorry for this, kid. Paybacks are a bitch."

"I ain't scared of you, kidnapper!" Robbie crowed, and stuck out his tongue.

Pocketknife swatted his mother aside, lunged, and took a handful of Robbie's shirt in his fist, simultaneously cocking his right arm back.

"This is for being a loudmouth," he said, punching the boy hard in the face.

Robbie screamed. Pocketknife felt his mother's hands claw at his back.

"And this is for being a brat," he growled, punching him again. He turned and hurled the boy against the refrigerator. The assemblage of magnets there popped free and ticked on the linoleum while various notes and papers and a shopping list fluttered down. Robbie slid to the floor.

"Percy!" Dottie Hursch shouted as Pocketknife lunged toward Robbie again and hauled him upright. She hurled herself against him and encircled his waist in a bear hug. "Stop it!"

Pocketknife shook her off. "This one's for good measure," he said and sent his fist crashing into Robbie's face again. His screams filled the room. Blood gushed out of his nose in twin rivulets, dripping off his chin. Pocketknife battered him, grinning, breathing through his mouth, unaware that his Salem was still clamped between his lips, the crawling smoke stinging his eyes.

"Percy!"

He turned his head, distracted, and saw a big, round, dark object swoop toward his head. He ducked instinctively, but too late.

The cast-iron skillet thudded down on his skull, spraying bacon grease against the ruined paint of the walls. Pocketknife staggered sideways, holding his head, biting back a scream of his own.

"Get out!" Dottie shrieked, lifting the heavy iron skillet with both hands. "Get out or I'll hit you again!"

Robbie slumped to the floor, clutching his face, sobbing.

For Pocketknife the world spun and swam. He squinted at his mother, the bedraggled, aging woman who had brought him into this world, into this hell. It occurred to him to kill her.

"Out," she said. "Now."

He pulled himself up straighter, jerked the cigarette out of his mouth, and flipped it across the kitchen. It hit the wall with a shower of sparks. "Screw you," he said. "Screw you all."

Reeling and stumbling, he made his way out.

Twenty minutes later Robbie Hursch looked up from the blood-spattered bathroom sink and saw in the mirror how badly his young face had been rearranged by his sadistic brother. His lips were cut and blackening. One eye was swollen to a glistening slit. His nose seemed to have grown to twice its normal size.

"Bastard Pocketshit Percy," he blubbered to his reflection. Tears coursed down his cheeks, and he dabbed them away with the bloody towel he held in his hands. "Bastard."

He dropped the towel in the sink, checked his reflection one more time, and went out into the hallway. At the end of it, on a small wooden table, was the telephone.

He detoured through the kitchen. Smashed plates still littered the floor. Bacon grease oozed down the walls in shiny strings. Outside, children laughed and screamed.

His mother had gone to her room after the fracas to get dressed.

The newspaper lay on the floor, the page with the huge black print beside it.

"Bastard," he whispered, picking it up.

He went to the telephone, envisioning Pocketknife's face when the cops came to ask him all sorts of questions. They might even take him to jail for a day or two while the lie was investigated. That would be paybacks. And paybacks were a bitch.

Grinning crookedly, he picked up the phone and dialed. It booped and beeped and clacked. Then someone answered.

"Serious calls only." The guy sounded out of breath.

"I have . . ." Robbie whispered. A sudden thought struck him: what would Pocketknife's paybacks be when he got out of jail? But would he really ever know who had pulled this trick on him? Could he prove it?

"Speak up," the man at the other end of the line said.

"I have information," Robbie said. His voice trembled, and he swallowed to make it stop. "About the kidnappings, like in the paper."

"Go on."

"My brother did it."

"Is this a kid speaking? Look, I've had my fill of these calls."

"No, really!" Robbie cupped his hand over the mouthpiece. "He's got a ton of money all of a sudden."

"So?"

"He steals it out of their pockets!"

"I hate to say this, kid," the voice said, "but take a hike."

The phone went dead.

Got to stay alive.

Flynn dragged himself forward as the sun peaked in the sky and began its gradual descent into afternoon, its hot rays filtering through the trees onto the weeds. He had been crawling for what seemed like days on end, his strength ebbing with every tortured movement, his blood languidly oozing out of his body just slowly enough to keep him from dying. Still he felt cold, though it had to be hot by now. The pain in his stomach was enormous. His shoulder muscles ached. The need for sleep was searing into his brain telling him to stop, to lie quietly and rest.

You do that, and you are a dead man.

When he found help, which he surely must do soon, he would tell the truth about Pocketknife and Fritz and that perverted bastard Hopewell. He had already made up his mind about that. He would tell about the kidnappings and the people celebrating in monks' robes at the fancy mansion where they danced the night away. With his frightful injuries he would be granted immunity from prosecution. He would take any deal they offered, would sell his own mother for the chance to live and be free. And yes, he would clean up his act and become a respectable human being, abandon crime, find a job, raise a family. This close to death, he was realizing the enormity of his slide into sin. So yes, he would even go to church, go there every frigging *day,* if only God would let him find help in these woods and these brambles, and let him live to see another sunrise.

He estimated he had crawled about half a mile. The terrain was uphill now, tougher even than before. He allowed himself a short pause, just long enough to catch his breath. He was shivering, his body electric with pain. His elbows were scraped raw, his Mensa shirt clotted with mud and sticking leaves. He knew there were roads here, had to be. He strained his ears, hoping to catch the sound of passing cars, but heard only the twitter of birds perched in the branches overhead. For a moment his eyes drifted shut and the need to sleep washed over him in warm, pleasant waves that promised to carry him away from the horror forever.

He jerked his eyes open, gritting his teeth against the urge to sleep. Let his ruined guts sleep, let them sleep and stop hurting. For all he cared, his nerveless legs could detach themselves and stomp off alone. He would not let his mind sleep until he found assistance and told the law everything he knew. To hell with a personal revenge; a man dead from the waist down needed better ways. That, he figured, is why there are laws. To help the innocent get revenge.

He dragged himself farther and found that he was at the edge of a small stream, more like a shallow ditch with some fairly clean water burbling past. He pressed his lips into it and was about to drink when an alarm went off in his mind.

What was he doing? He had never been in the military, but you don't grow up watching war movies without finding out quick that if you've been shot or stabbed in the stomach, the last thing you need is water. Sure, wounded men were always thirsty, but the medics in the movies never let them drink water or anything else. So, instead, Flynn crawled through it. It felt as cold as winter slush. He began to shiver violently, and worked his way into a patch of sunlight where he paused, gasping. A look behind him showed that he had tinged the water with small, dissipating whirlpools of blood.

A terrible fear surged through him. He had been bleeding for hours; Christ, maybe it really had been days by now. He was lost and alone in a woods that could stretch for a dozen miles or more. Who was he kidding?

Nobody, he decided. It was, at long last, time to die.

He closed his eyes, and in that brief moment of darkness he saw Norman Hopewell in his ghastly red robe, lifting a glimmering knife, plunging it downward.

His eyes popped open. Even in his dying moment, he was to be tortured.

He crawled away, too scared to give up.

Robbie Hursch stared at the phone. His face hurt really bad. The inside of his mouth was still bleeding, giving everything a salty taste. He could barely see out of his right eye. "Bastard Pocketknife," he said to himself, holding the receiver at his chest, unsure whether to try again or not. Mom would yell if she found out, but as mad as she was, maybe she'd think it was a great practical joke on Percy. And even if she spanked him, Robbie knew it would hurt a hell of a lot less than Percy's beating did.

He dialed the phone again. It rang five times, six.

"Hello. All callers are advised that the use of this number for purposes other than relating pertinent information will be prosecuted to the fullest extent of the law."

Robbie frowned. What had he said?

"Hello?" the man repeated. "Hello? Jesus Christ . . ."

Clunk.

Robbie licked his swollen lips, unsure now. He heard something thump and hurriedly reassembled the phone, afraid that his mother might catch him, but she didn't.

He eyed the phone. How could they prosecute you if they didn't even know who you were? Somebody was trying to scare him. He checked the number and dialed again.

"What!"

The guy sure was crabby, Robbie decided. "Listen up," he snarled. "You hang up on me again and I ain't calling back, and I know who you're looking for."

Silence, for a time. Then: "Are you the kid who just called?"

"Maybe so, maybe not so."

Click!

Robbie grinned. This was going to be tough. Thank God it wasn't long distance. He dialed again.

"Hot goddamn line."

"My brother Percy is the kidnapper," Robbie said, "and I can prove it."

"Aren't you the same kid who just called me twice?"

"No, sir. My mother just now asked me to call."

"Then let me speak to her."

Robbie hesitated. "Uh, she has laryngitis."

A sigh. A click.

Robbie rubbed his face. He checked the paper and dialed again.

It was answered fast. "Kid, why are you doing this to me?"

"Because my brother *is* the guy who kidnapped all those people. I am an eyewitness."

Another sigh. "Your name, then?"

Robbie smiled. "I ain't gonna tell you that just yet. I want Percy arrested first."

"Hmmm." There was a long pause full of breathing. Then the crabby man said, "Tell me about Percy."

"Okay. Percy is a big stupid creep who hasn't had a job for about a year, but now he's got all kinds of money in an envelope. He says he drives a truck."

"Maybe he does."

"Getting up any time he wants and partying all night? He's so drunk most of the time he's either passed out or throwing up. What company wants a driver like that?"

More breathing. "What does he drink?"

"I don't know. Mostly my mom's vodka when she can't afford anything better."

"This is pretty skimpy information. Don't you know anything else?"

Robbie thought it over, afraid of losing this opportunity to really hit Percy where it hurt. "I know one thing," he said. "When he saw that reward offer in the paper he got as white as a sheet and started to sweat real bad. Then I teased him about it, and he got so crazy that my mom had to hit him with a skillet to keep him from trying to kill me."

"All right, kid. Give me your name and address and I might swing by."

"Sure." Robbie mentally rubbed his hands with glee, hoping Percy would be back just in time. "I live at forty-four eighty-one West Washington. You go down Forty-third Street till it curves, and then you—"

A shadow darkened the hallway, blotting out the sunlight, falling across Robbie and the telephone on the little wooden stand. Robbie turned his head slowly, scared, certain that it was . . .

Pocketknife.

"Hang up, you little bastard," Pocketknife demanded huskily. Blood was dripping down his ear from his scalp. He was as pale as hot ashes, his face twisted up into something almost too ugly to recognize. He had become a monster.

The phone dropped from Robbie's hand and clunked on the floor.

"Hello!" Darkman shouted from his end of the line. "Hello! Are you there?"

All he heard were things crashing and banging. Then someone began to scream.

CHAPTER

16

Some Shady Plans

It was just past one-thirty when the front door of the mansion swung open and Fritz walked in with a big grin on his sallow face. He found Hopewell in the kitchen heating up a TV dinner and writing something on a sheet of paper while the room filled with the flat, factory-cooked aroma of chicken and potatoes.

"Got 'em," Fritz said, and sat down.

Hopewell looked up. "Got what?"

"Forty-four rifles."

"How much did they cost?"

"You don't want to know."

Hopewell shrugged and went back to his writing.

Fritz eyed the sheet of paper. "Writing your memoirs?"

"Nope." Hopewell erased a word and brushed the detritus away. "Tonight's special sermon."

"No ad-libbing this time?"

"This sermon is too important. It will make us or break us. How does this sound? 'The backbone of mankind, the thing that pulled him from the mud of the savage primordial swamps into mastery of the world, has been his dedication to oneness, his sense of holy unity.'"

Fritz made faces as he digested it. "Only one problem. We didn't crawl out of any mud, according to the faith. God made us in his own image—zap, bang, boom."

"Oops. Screwed that one up." He bent to his writing again.

"Also, if people are so damn unified as a species, how come we go to war every few years and blow each other up?"

Hopewell glanced up at him. "You're a malcontent. Did you get bullets?"

"Ten shells for each gun. So now, who are we supposed to shoot at? Who's the enemy?"

Hopewell put the pencil down. "Everybody else in the world is our enemy. It's us against the others. And especially us against our traitors. Classic xenophobia is my goal."

Fritz scowled. "Which phobia is that one?"

"A phobic hatred of foreigners. During a war they call it patriotism. Men go to their death fighting foreigners. They get posthumous medals killing them. If they shoot foreigners in peacetime, they get arrested. What planet have you been living on all these years?"

"Now *you* sound like a malcontent. How do you feel about shotguns?"

"Huh?"

"Shotguns cost a whole lot less than regular rifles, especially the ones made by companies nobody's ever heard of."

"Will they fire?"

Fritz raised his shoulders. "For sixty bucks each they ought to. Plus tax."

Hopewell frowned. "Only sixty bucks? What gauge are they?"

"Four-ten. You got a problem with that?"

"Four-ten? That's something you'd buy for a nine-year-old kid!"

"But you can kill somebody with one, that's a fact."

"Sure, if you jam it in his mouth before you pull the trigger."

"Don't tell me," Fritz said darkly, "that you want me to take them all back."

Hopewell shook his head. "We don't have anybody to shoot at anyway. It's the impression we create that matters, not the firepower. Besides, a real shotgun would be too heavy for those old people to carry. Hey, how does this sound? It just popped into my head. 'Loyalty to our leader, loyalty to ourselves, loyalty to our god.' "

"Wonderful. I notice you come first."

"You bet your ass I do." He got up and went to the oven, where steamy heat was battling with the air conditioning. "We need to get a microwave," Hopewell complained. "So how much is forty-four times sixty?"

"Close to three grand. Tack on another hundred for the bullets."

"Shells."

"Whatever. Where should we put the damn things?"

Hopewell came back and sat again. "Anywhere in the house is good enough. Just try to bring them in quietly." He picked up the pencil. "I need to concentrate."

"So," Fritz said, "I get to do the grunt work again?"

He nodded. "You the brawn, me the brains. You'd better get on the phone and start summoning the faithful to tonight's gathering. We've got to have every single member here. And remember, the defiling will be a freebie this time."

"I don't think that's wise." Fritz aimed his thumb over his shoulder, motioning to the driveway. "We've got to make up the cash for the guns and the ammo. How about we make the ceremony half-price? They'll go for it."

"Sure, fine. Just get busy."

As Fritz went out into the heat to empty the U-Haul van, it came to him that with all these guns around, somebody might get accidentally shot. And wouldn't that be hard to explain to the grieving family? Well, that wasn't his problem anymore. He had no problems at all anymore. This afternoon, between trips to various sporting goods stores and gun shops, he had stopped at a travel agency called Global Express. The planes to Rio this time of year weren't nearly as crowded as in the winter, and he got a window seat in first class for less than six hundred dollars one-way. And that was all he needed.

Because by the time the insanity was in full swing tonight, he would be kicked back with a martini in one hand and an in-flight magazine in the other, winging his way toward the ultimate vacationer's paradise while Hopewell and his daffy followers caroused and partied. Defiling little girls was ugly enough, but Fritz had learned to live with it. Sacrificing a man on the defilement altar had been his own desperate idea, but he wasn't stupid enough to hang around and face murder charges for *that* brainstorm.

Tonight's proceeds would go directly into his pocket. This was what had stopped him before, the fact that Hopewell controlled all the money; he knew he would have to risk waiting for another ceremony, then quickly scoop up the profits and run. Hopewell's idea of presenting another defilement so soon after the last one was perfect, the only real brainstorm he'd ever had.

At Global Express, Fritz had used his newest alias, which he hoped would be his name for the rest of his life, or until he had to run again: Emerson Paul Freemont—same initials as Edgar P. Fritz.

He carted the shotguns in, wondering how to say "a room for one" in Portuguese, the language of romantic Brazil.

CHAPTER

17

Massacre

Darkman slammed the phone down, his thoughts in chaos. The kid who called—that was no joke. He had to go there to check it out.

He jogged to the front door, remembering as he pushed through into the sunlight that he had been ready to shuck his chief-of-police face when the phone rang and he was interrupted. The skin was still holding together, though he had little idea how long it had been alive so far. It was a risk he would have to live with. That kid, whoever he was, had gotten someone highly agitated by calling the hot line. An internal family spat at 4481 West Washington, or a rock-solid lead? Maybe neither.

Maybe both.

As the door of the soap factory banged shut behind him, he regretted the fact that he did not have a car. Usually he went nowhere and didn't miss the luxury of wheels. On the rare times that he did go out, he either walked or took a cab. So far no real emergency had popped up.

Until now. He stood in the sunlight breathing the fetid air of this rotten core of the old city. Did taxis ever come here? Not unless he called them. How often did winos and street bums have the dough for a cab? As good as never.

Clenching his fists with helplessness, breathing hard, he pulled up a mental map and searched for West Washington. It cut through the western hindquarter of town out by the railyards that dead-ended at the riverfront loading docks. Estimated distance? Eleven miles, give or take. He would have to call Julie. Her, or a taxi. Either way it would take precious time, time that kid might not have to spare. He whirled around, his false face drawn up with irritation, but a distant motion caught his eye. He turned again.

A car was coming down the dirty street, moving in and out of the shadows cast by the dead hulks of abandoned buildings. Hallelujah. It was a big red sedan, a Cadillac or Grand Marquis. The license plate screwed to the shiny front bumper told Darkman that this car was from the Hoosier state of Indiana, a state most of Darkman's acquaintances didn't want to be from. Here we have, he thought, a tourist from cornfield country, lost in the big bad city. He waved his arms over his head, thumping his skull with the bones of his forearms in his excitement. Dressed like this, looking as dignified as this, he thought the driver would surely stop for him.

He was right. With a small squeal of the brakes the car—a Caddy indeed—pulled up beside him and stopped. The smell of hot new auto parts drifted up; this baby was fresh out of the showroom back home. It was piloted by an overweight fellow in a flashy red sport coat. Through the driver's mirrored sunglasses Darkman saw only his own reflection, the chief of police loitering in this urban ghost town. Fortunately the guy was not from around here.

"Hey, mister!" the driver called out. "How in the heck does a man get out of this slum and back onto U.S. Seventy-six?"

Darkman put his hands on the upper frame of the

door. "I'm an undercover cop. I need to borrow your car."

The man frowned, looking both stupid and alarmed. He peeled his sunglasses off. "Huh?"

Darkman jerked the door open. "Get out. Police business."

"Now hold on a second," he bleated. "Cops don't do this kind of stuff, not where I come from. Show me some I.D."

Darkman clamped a hand around his throat. "Out, dammit!"

"Now wait!" The color was draining out of the tourist's chubby face. "This is more like a carjacking!"

"It's exactly like a carjacking," Darkman snarled, and dragged him out.

The driver fell to his knees on the hot asphalt. His sunglasses skittered away and clicked on the curb.

"Help! Police! He's stealing my car!"

Darkman climbed inside, slammed the door shut, and rammed the gearshift into reverse. The Cadillac roared backward with a screech, the big engine howling out its indignation. As he downshifted, the fat man got up and charged at him. He began to hammer on the hood with his fists, squalling like a prime Indiana heifer at the county fair.

"You're getting on my nerves," Darkman muttered, unable to drive because the guy was in front of the car. As he jumped out to tell him to get the hell away, his nose caught a whiff of familiar smoke.

His face was croaking. Yellow strings dripped on his suit coat like melting taffy. Smoke billowed around him in a fine yellow cloud. The man from the corn belt eyeballed him with stunned horror, frozen in position.

"Rrraaaahhh!" Darkman shrieked at him.

It was enough to make Arnold Schwarzenegger himself run screaming down the street. Never had Darkman seen a man that fat move quite that fast. His screams could have been recorded for use in a scary movie. "Goddamn tourist," Darkman grumbled, and scurried back into the car. He made the engine howl and peeled out in a tight circle accompanied by a cloud of dense blue Goodyear smoke, forming a new map in his mind with a giant flashing X where he would find 4481 West Washington and a kid very likely in bad trouble, a kid whose name he did not even know.

Osgood Flynn could crawl no more.

In his fevered mind he was able to congratulate himself on a battle well fought, but it brought little consolation. He had been stabbed more times than your average pin cushion, his spine was likely severed, he had not slept for an eternity, and it was colder than a polar bear's nose on this wintry summer day, and his determination was gone. He had lived a dangerous life, had played a dangerous game, had lost. He had done everything possible to make his upper-class family disown him, had worked overtime at being worthless. As a reward, he was suffering and would soon die, alone, abandoned.

He was panting heavily, his face pressed into the stiff, scratchy weeds of this dense no-man's-land. He had always thought that this area where the mansions were nested on the hilltops was a haven for the filthy rich, teeming with stuffed shirts and political types. But this was like another planet, this trackless woods filled with cackling bugs and birds. It seemed likely that he had been dumped far, far away from Hopewell's house of horrors after all. He wondered if he had crawled in circles. He wondered if he had crawled one inch and imagined all the rest.

He was lying beside a tall tree whose branches cast dappled sunlight across his back, warming him slightly. His shivering had set in so deep he thought he must surely hear his bones begin to rattle. With effort he raised his head. Dead leaves stuck to his face, which was scratched and bleeding from an encounter with a brier bush. With difficulty he focused his bleary eyes.

He saw trees, weeds, a yellow flower with pink fringes poking up from the ground. Never big on flowers, he didn't know this one from a Venus's-flytrap, but it was pretty. In a life of ugliness, perhaps only death could bring beauty.

He dragged himself toward it. His elbows dug ruts in the damp ground as he grunted his way along. His shoulders ached like the joints of a man stricken with arthritis. The miasma of pain in his abdomen had been so overwhelming for so long that he could have dragged himself over barbed wire and felt nothing new. Surely no one could experience this much pain without either dying or going insane. And maybe this last doomed trek toward a useless forest flower was insanity.

Something was impeding his progress, holding him back. With a shuddering gasp he gave up and waited for death. It wouldn't be so bad. Just to drift off, give in to that urge to sleep that beckoned to him like a soft and beautiful woman, just beyond his reach and his sight.

He let his face fall to the ground. He smelled damp leaves and mulch and the dirt beneath. To die, and be buried in the earth. Eternal relief. Eternal rest. If only he could die.

Something snapped in the woods off to his right. Something shuffled through the leaves.

Flynn raised his head. His neckbones creaked and crackled, the neckbones of a dying man. He saw a world of fuzzy green striped with the brown shafts of saplings. With effort, he brought the scene into focus.

Sticks cracked and broke. Leaves whispered against each other. Flynn turned his head. His tortured neck creaked again like an old hinge. He squinted, half expecting to see a woman dressed in white, the angel of death looking for him in this forsaken wasteland.

He saw nothing. The noise was fading away.

"Help," Flynn whispered. His tongue was too big and swollen in his mouth to let more than a squeak escape past it. His dry throat ached.

The noise was going, far to the right. Flynn followed it with his eyes, trying to form words.

The path behind him, where he had crawled through

the brush caught his eye, and the words died in his mouth.

A rope of intestine, gray-white and bloody, had snagged on a clump of briers some yards away and had been unreeling as he crawled. With a great burst of energy he rolled over and rose up on his battered elbows, looking down at himself.

His severed guts were hanging out from all directions. He saw his own liver, bloated with the foamy yellow fat of alcoholic hepatitis, flecked with grime.

His eyes grew huge in his head. He knew that he owed no revenge to anyone in the world because *this* was *their* revenge. He had gutted an innocent man and kidnapped his daughter, and as punishment, God had gutted *him*.

He wrenched his mouth open. "Aaaahhhhhhh! Aaaahhhhhhhhh!"

Now the noises came closer again. As Flynn screamed in horror and agony he coughed a huge purple blot of congealed blood out of his mouth. It slithered wetly down his chest to plop into the hollow of his belly as a long, misty blurt of fresh red blood spurted from his gaping mouth and sprayed out beyond his feet.

By the time the lady who had been strolling through the woods on this fine afternoon got to him and began to scream, Osgood Flynn was dead. The coroner would later remark that if he hadn't known better, he could have sworn, from the look on the young man's face, that he had died not of multiple stab wounds but of terror.

Darkman careened through the sparse afternoon traffic, the Cadillac's big horn blowing a rapid machine-gun beat as he ran through red lights and shot past stop signs. The Caddy was as heavy as a tank, the ultra-tuned suspension absorbing the potholes and cracks while barely rocking the chassis. Hokey country music was crooning out of hidden speakers. The car had less than a thousand miles on it, but already it smelled like a cigarette factory inside. Even so, the aroma of the

Indianan's bad habit was nothing compared to the stink of the artificial skin as it disintegrated. Darkman rolled a window down to let the smoke out, manipulating the electric controls to make the other windows open and shut in a slow-motion frenzy. When he punched the stereo controls, the music died, but the skin of his hand slurped off and stuck to the knobs to drip on the luxurious red carpeting.

He spied a street sign: West Jefferson. All of the presidentially named streets were clustered here, most of them flanked by tenement buildings and housing projects speckled with broken windows. He zipped through the intersections at Jefferson, at Madison, at Roosevelt. The next one was Washington. Cutting a hard left while the tires howled, he cut off a pickup and sent it crashing against the curb. A huge spout of water geysered into the air as the truck knocked a hydrant over. Angry shouts followed Darkman away. He looked for numbers on the buildings, saw 3255, then 3310. He was going the right way; the numbers were getting bigger. When he checked the speedometer as he whipped through another red light, he discovered he was going sixty-five. Wait a second. Why kill someone on the road for an elaborate prank?

He slowed down, glad that no cops were on his tail yet. The house numbers grew as the newer buildings gave way to projects and then some tenements. He saw an ancient caving-in building whose front door bore traces of missing numbers: 4481.

He jammed on the brakes and threw the gearshift into park.

Noticing a knot of kids jammed around the front door, Darkman climbed out of the car and hurried across the grassless yard. Some of the kids were standing on tiptoe, peeking through the first-floor windows, jabbering excitedly.

"Move away from the door," he said, and they turned. With a few horrified screams they scattered. He went up the crumbling stoop that led to the front door, crouching a bit, moving cautiously as he approached another door, not at all aware that he looked like the Grim Reaper in a business suit.

The apartment door was ajar. He touched it and it swung open. A smell wafted out, easy enough to identify —bacon. The whole place reeked of bacon.

He stepped inside and swept the inner hallway with his eyes. To his right, through an open door, he saw a living room: furniture, a sofa with the stuffing oozing out of a dozen holes, an ancient coffee table with an empty vase on it, an upended lamp in one corner.

A body was sprawled on the floor at the end of the hall. He hurried forward and knelt beside it. It was a young black boy, perhaps ten or eleven, obviously dead. His face was an unrecognizable lump of bloody flesh, and his neck was broken. The kid was lying on his stomach, but his head had been twisted around to face the ceiling. One dead eye stared balefully at Darkman's left ear; the other eye was puffed shut.

Darkman stood up, his stomach cold and uneasy. Flies buzzed in the stillness. An overturned table blocked the hallway. A telephone lay in jagged pieces beside it. Blood glistened on the receiver, and Darkman suddenly knew what had turned the boy's face into a broken mask: he had been killed with the phone.

Darkman's newspaper ad was a crumpled ball beside the table; there was a spray of blood on it. The hallway ended in a brightly sunlit kitchen where a furry pink slipper lay in a square of sunlight.

He stepped over the telephone stand and walked into the kitchen. The smell of bacon was stronger here. He saw grease splattered all over one wall. Papers and refrigerator magnets were strewn on the floor. The kitchen table was overturned. Dishes had been smashed everywhere.

A dead woman lay beside the refrigerator. Her head looked as if someone had pounded it in a frenzy with a bat or club. Bits of bone, like broken piano keys, protruded from the bloody mat of her hair. Both of her eyes had popped out of their sockets from the force of the blows. Her tongue stuck out of her dead mouth. A fly ambled across it.

He saw blood and patches of skin under her finger-nails: she hadn't given up without a fight, so someone was marked by some bloody gashes now.

Hearing a movement in an adjoining room, he shoved open a small door. It banged into the wall, then swung back and forth on squeaking hinges.

"Stay away!" someone screamed from inside the room.

Darkman looked in. A wave of revulsion passed across the remains of his face. The dimly lit room contained only a bed.

A man was standing on it holding a heavy cast-iron skillet with both hands. Blood and clots of flesh dripped from it onto the sheets. Blood was sprayed across his T-shirt and face. His brown hair was twisted into sweaty knots. Deep bleeding gashes had been slashed across his face in crisscrossing lines.

"Percy?" Darkman said.

The man bared his teeth in an animal snarl. "You can't prove nothing!" he shrieked, and hurled the skillet at him. Darkman ducked. The frying pan hit the door with a loud bang, spattering the paint with blood.

"Talk to me, Percy," Darkman said as evenly as he could amid this carnage.

"She screwed everybody!" he screamed. Tears seeped out of his eyes and tracked down his bloody cheeks. "She sold herself. But I took care of the kid. I messed him up bad! Hah!"

"Be very calm," Darkman said. "I'm here to help."

"There's no help for me," Percy said miserably. "I never said I was Mensa material anyway." He jerked suddenly, as if something had struck him. His eyes grew huge and he lifted a finger to point at Darkman. "You're the face of death!" he shrieked in terror. "You can't take me!"

He jammed a hand into his pocket. Darkman crouched a bit, ready to jump away if a gun appeared.

Instead, Percy withdrew an envelope and fanned the air with it. Suddenly money was fluttering through the room.

"Take it!" Percy said, flapping the envelope. "Just don't take me!"

He reached into his other pocket and pulled out a large knife. He flicked it with a twist of his hand, and the blade clicked out. "You'll never prove a thing," he said with sullen, childish petulance.

He reached up and sliced open his own throat. The spurt of blood from his severed jugular was immediate and huge, a thick cascade that gushed down his chest. He made gagging noises. Darkman realized he was trying to scream.

"Jesus Christ," Darkman whispered.

He watched as the life squirted out of the man named Percy, who sank to his knees on the bed, then to his haunches, still flapping money out of the envelope. He seemed to grin at some secret joke. Then he toppled off the bed. His head hit an empty vodka bottle and sent it spinning.

A fifty-dollar bill pinwheeled down and landed on his dead and grinning face.

And in the distance: sirens.

CHAPTER

18

Funus Interruptus

Julie had always loathed funerals, but this one would be especially ghastly. At the head of the room two coffins rested on draped biers, surrounded by flowers from grieving friends, co-workers, and relatives. Julie sat in the section reserved for family members in this big Smythe-Mulcahey funeral home, one of the city's finest, a luxury Julie's heartsick mother had demanded.

Suitably depressing religious music was being piped in, and the smell of flowers was thick and hideously sweet. Julie was wearing a somber brown dress, a veiled hat, and white gloves, the usual mourning costume worn during funeral services. If Jerry were here as an observer instead of the honored guest, she thought crazily, he would crank up some rock and roll music and pop open a cooler full of beer. But Jerry was dead, at age thirty-three. It seemed impossible.

Both coffins were closed, mercifully. There had been a private viewing, but Julie had declined to see Jerry and Margaret that way, knowing that if the situation were reversed, she would expect the same courtesy. She did not know if there was a heaven or a hell, but if she ever saw her brother and his wife again, the reunion would be more pleasant without the mental image of their bloodless corpses lingering in her spiritual mind.

Pretty heavy thinking, she decided as she waited in dread for the funeral to start. Jerry and Margaret had not been religious people, so the minister selected to lead the service was a stranger. Little Tina was not in attendance, though Julie's mother had wanted her to come.

By now most of the mourners were seated, whispering while they waited for the service to get under way. Time droned on. Julie was clutching a Kleenex that she was determined not to use. Her mother, seated to her left, was crying enough for both of them. To her right sat Martin Clayborne, holding her squirming hand in his firm and reassuring one. When this was over, Julie would be reprimanded by her mother for inviting a mere boyfriend to sit in the family section. So what? When she had buried Peyton her mother had not shown up to support her. In fact, Jerry had offered only obligatory condolences. In the Hastings family, boyfriends ranked right down there with annoying acquaintances, nosy neighbors, and bill collectors.

A movement caught her eye, and she watched as Detective Sam Weatherspoon breezed in and began looking around. His expression was cool and detached until he spied Julie. He started toward her with his suit coat open and the pistol on his belt visible between strides. He was apparently not here to pay his respects.

Julie got to her feet. Martin looked up at her, a question in his eyes. She nodded toward Weatherspoon, and he looked around. "Christ," he grumbled, and stood up. "Nothing can be this important."

Weatherspoon vanished behind a purple velvet curtain and reemerged in the family section. Julie and Martin met him and pressed him back toward the farthest wall, signaling annoyance with their eyes.

He raised his hands. "I have questions that can't wait," he whispered. "I told the preacher to stall for a while."

Martin touched his forehead, eyeing Weatherspoon. "I don't believe this."

"Believe it." He looked at Julie. "On the night that you were set on fire, we took samples of various substances found at the scene. The strangest, besides the headless body and gallons of blood, was a lot of weird goo splattered around. It felt like rubber when we bagged it, but within a few hours it had turned to yellow dust. It smelled real bad, like burning tires. Our lab identified it as a combination of unusual chemicals that didn't make sense. They sent it on to the FBI labs in Virginia."

Julie listened wordlessly while Martin shifted impatiently from foot to foot.

"The FBI technicians worked on it, tried to rehydrate it, dumped it inside some kind of million-dollar machine, and let it simmer. They too got a mixture of chemicals that didn't make sense, so they heated it back to liquid and zapped electricity through it."

Julie swallowed. This sounded too familiar. Martin flapped his hands. "Okay, Weatherspoon, surprise us and leave us alone."

He nodded almost imperceptibly. "When they zapped it, it became goo."

"This isn't funny," Martin growled.

"Very strange goo," Weatherspoon went on. "It seemed to be alive. Artificial skin. Ninety-nine minutes later it died again."

Julie felt her knees wobble.

Weatherspoon pressed on. "It's common enough knowledge that Peyton Westlake was working on just such a project when his lab exploded and he was killed. Isn't that right?"

Julie nodded.

"No one ever found his body and within a week a lot of unsavory people began to die," Weatherspoon went on, relieving her of the task of replying. His lime-green eyes were flashing. "Suddenly, known hoods began falling out of skyscrapers under construction, falling out of high-rise apartment buildings, popping up out of manholes and getting mooshed, being ripped to shreds by shotguns, blown to bits in helicopter explosions . . . shall I go on?"

Julie felt faint. The music floating through the room was horrible, her brother was inside a box for all eternity, her boyfriend was hearing things she never wanted him to hear. She had indeed told him about the explosion, and that Peyton was presumed dead and preferred it that way, but she had not mentioned the artificial skin or the fact that Peyton could be just about anyone he wanted to be and do terrible things . . . like kill people.

Martin exhaled heavily. "If you've got a point, please make it. This is not the best of times for Julie."

"Sure." Weatherspoon's lips curved in a small, tight arc. "It looks like Julie's ex-fiancé is alive and well and very, very dangerous."

Through her daze of shock she heard Martin's voice rise. "I happen to know that Julie has neither seen nor heard from her former fiancé and that to her knowledge he is very, very dead."

"He saved her life," Weatherspoon retorted nastily. "And she knows it."

Martin snorted. "This is absurd. Julie was on fire, man, *on fire!* I would not care if Charles Manson himself put that fire out!"

"Westlake doused her in human blood, Mr. Clayborne, after ripping her assailant's head off!"

Martin straightened. "That is impossible."

"Not for him."

"He's dead and buried."

"Just one ear in the ground. One ear."

"Are you here to charge Julie with a crime?"

"No," he answered easily. "I just want to know where her boyfriend is hiding and what he looks like under that artificial skin."

Julie knew that Peyton could look like anybody he wanted, but that was his special secret. She would not deprive him of that.

"I take it, then," Martin said, "that you don't have anything to report about Julie's kidnapped niece."

Now Weatherspoon's gaze faltered. "Not unless we can tie her disappearance to Westlake somehow. He knew where the family lived."

"So did the mailman."

"The mailman doesn't go around ripping people's heads off," Weatherspoon barked. Mourners turned to look. "He doesn't throw his enemies out of tall buildings. He doesn't make artificial skin, and he doesn't impersonate people."

Martin chuckled evilly. "So you intend to arrest a dead man for impersonating people?"

Julie moaned. "Oh, just stop it." This was insane. The room was getting hot, too hot and cramped, and these two were scrapping like terriers. "I can't talk about this right now. I can't . . ."

She slumped against Martin's shoulder, wishing she could faint but knowing she wouldn't.

"I think you've done your job," Martin hissed, moving to support some of Julie's weight and keep her upright. "Now may we pay our last respects to her brother and his wife?"

Weatherspoon shook his head, shrugged. "Sometimes I get carried away," he murmured, and walked off.

Martin guided Julie back to her seat.

"Thanks," she was able to whisper as she sat down.

"That guy is a jerk," he said darkly. "And you don't need to thank me for a thing."

She rested her forehead against his shoulder just as the minister strode to the lectern. "I mean thanks for backing me up about Peyton. You know as well as I do that he's alive."

He nodded, then whispered in her ear. "Let's just get through this ordeal, and you can tell me what's *really* going on—if you want to. *Only* if you want to."

"I will," she promised, and the minister began to

speak while her mother sobbed and somewhere in the back a baby began to cry. The funeral wasn't any less painful than the interrogation had been, and she still had the burial to face, and the reception afterward at her apartment, where she would be expected to eat and drink and be as close to merry as she could get.

CHAPTER

19

No Laughing Matter

The phone was ringing when Darkman opened the door of the factory that had once employed scores of people but was now an abandoned hulk full of useless machinery and broken hopes. He was tired and demoralized, looked like a walking escapee from a wax museum, a modern-day Frankenstein, star of the monster section that housed other notables such as the Mummy and the Wolfman, Dracula and Freddy Krueger. Darkman pushed the door shut and walked inside while his eyes adjusted to the dimness.

He went to his bank of computers and fell into his battered chair while the phone rang and rang and rang. He had found the key that would have solved the crime, but now the little kid and the mother and the kidnapper were all dead. Percy had been a man eaten alive with guilt. If only he had stayed alive long enough to explain what had happened to the kidnapped girls.

Ring. Ring.

To hell with the phone. Darkman remembered with a good deal of chagrin how he had tried to catch some of the kids who had been gawking on the stoop. He had wanted to ask them some questions, but he'd caused a near-riot instead. At least he hadn't needed to call the cops and ask them to question the kids, get them to explain the situation, because the cops were already there and all of those kids would be interrogated. Also, Darkman had had no desire to stick around to be asked a series of unanswerable questions, especially looking the way he did. A messy murder like that, him hanging around without a face—it would have made the papers, even in this town, which was infamous for its gruesome murders. It would even have been grist for the TV tabloid shows—lots of sensational, gory murders committed by loved ones upon loved ones, and by the way, who was that walking skeleton we saw?

And so he sat and listened to the phone ring and ring. He did not care if Elvis himself was calling to report that he was alive and slinging burgers at an Arkansas truck stop. The best lead he would ever get had come from a little kid who was now dead because he had snitched on his brother.

The phone stopped ringing. Darkman accepted the fact with relief, but still sat with his bony chin propped on one bony fist, feeling tired enough to take a long nap. There was nothing else left to do.

The phone rang again. Darkman eyeballed it, envisioning himself shattering the phone into a million pieces.

Instead he leaned forward and picked it up. "Yes?" he said tiredly, defeated.

"Is this the reward line?" It was a woman. She was after the reward. Who wasn't?

"It is," he said.

"I've been calling for a long time," she said. "I have no idea if this has anything to do with those kidnappings. All I know is that I found a body, and I sure as hell am not going to report it to the cops before I report it to you. You're not the cops, correct?"

He yawned. "Correct."

"Will I get in trouble for calling you instead of them?"

He shrugged. "I'll never tell, lady, as long as you don't. What about this body?"

"It's the body of a young man," she said. She was reciting this as if she had rehearsed it while waiting for the phone to be answered. At least, he felt, she was being honest about her intentions. The chances that the body she'd found, if she really had found one, had anything to do with the kidnappings were very slim. Very. But they still existed.

"He looks about twenty," she went on. "I found him in the woodlands in the area of Centre Pointe, on a slope in the Kallares region."

Darkman took a breath. "Where might that be?"

"It's where all the mansions are, at the northern rim of the city. The mayor lives up that way."

"Got it." He picked up a pencil and began to bounce the eraser end on the table. After this call he was going to cut the phone line. To hell with the whole doomed project.

"He was murdered," she said. "Like they say in the papers, it was a grisly murder. He had been stabbed repeatedly. In the stomach."

"Uh-huh." People were stabbing each other like crazy lately. One man had recently knifed his wife sixty-one times because he didn't like the way she kept rearranging the food in the refrigerator.

"He had apparently dragged himself a long way down the side that slopes a lot. Otherwise I don't think he would have made it ten feet. Uphill, not an inch."

"Uh-huh."

"He has a lot of tattoos on his arms. That might be important."

"It might."

"He looks like he might have been tortured or something. His face is scary to look at, and his guts are strewn all over the place."

A disgusted sigh.

"Does any of that ring a bell?"

"I'm afraid not, ma'am. All of the kidnap victims have

146

been female and very young, and besides, there is no evidence that any of them were murdered. I'm afraid it doesn't fit at all."

"Unrelated, then?"

"Absolutely."

"So I should call the cops and forget about the money?"

"Afraid so, unless you've got something more solid. More . . . connecting evidence."

This time she sighed. "Well, ah, do you know if there's a Mensa Society in town? Just out of curiosity."

He jerked. "What?"

"The guy's wearing a shirt that has the words "Mensa Material" in big black letters on the front. The shirt's all chewed up and bloody from being stabbed so many times, but I could still read it."

He found that his heart was pounding. Percy had mentioned something about not being Mensa material before he slit his throat—a very odd thing to say by way of last words. Was it coincidence or a solid lead? "I don't know if there's a local chapter," he said. "All I know is you have to have a high IQ to join."

"So they say."

"Right. Now listen, please. Give me your name and address. I want to see this body."

"It's still out in the woods, and I'm home. Sometimes I jog up that way because the air's so much cleaner. Can you meet me here at my house?"

"You bet I can," he said, and used the pencil this time not for bouncing around to kill time, but to write down her name and address.

"Sixty-one Marigold Lane."

That was what it said on the mailbox, and that was what it said on the note in his hand. Darkman pulled the red Caddy up to the curb and checked his face in the rearview mirror. He did not like what he saw. The face of Jackson Goodrow, chief of police, stared back at him with disapproval. He had chosen to be the chief again rather than to use another of the faces in permanent machine language on hard disk, such as Peyton Westlake (dead), Robert Durant (dead), a guy named Ice (dead), Stryker (dead), or Smiley or Paulie or Martinez or Rick. Darkman was not in the mood to masquerade as a corpse. For once, he wanted to look like a basically nice guy, somebody you'd like to see your daughter bring home to supper.

Just don't step on his foot or spill gravy down his lap; he gets pissed.

"Funny ha-ha," he muttered as he climbed out of the Caddy's air-conditioned luxury and into the heat. The woman—one Darla Dalton, if she wasn't lying—was watching him from behind the door of 61 Marigold Lane, and he waved to her. She came out, and he almost fell over.

She was gorgeous. Shockingly black hair tumbling past her shoulders, her skin creamy and white and flawless, her smiling eyes a vivid shade of green. Her body was thin in the right places, padded in the others. He guessed she was about twenty-eight. She was wearing eyeglasses and was clad in a tight red dress.

But his on-again, off-again inner voice had something to say: *Forget it, buddy.*

He forgot it. Instead of hustling around to open the car door for her, he got back into the driver's seat as she climbed inside and she stared into his face.

"You're a cop after all!" she said, slamming her door. "I've seen your picture in the papers!"

"Family resemblance," he said. "Me and the chief are brothers."

"Then you're a P.I."

"Pacific island?"

She giggled, but not in a silly teenage way. "Make a U-turn," she said, motioning, "and follow the road that winds up into the mountains."

He did, and found, as he brought the car up to speed, that he was tongue-tied. It reminded him of his high school days and that memorable time when one of the senior cheerleaders had said hi to him in the hall. Peyton "the Weenie" Westlake had almost suffered a coronary.

"So are you a P.I.?" she asked.

Her perfume was wafting into his artificial nose. Very nice. "More like a concerned citizen," he said.

"Who's offering the reward? You?"

He nodded. "This road? Take a right here?"

"Yes." She settled back more comfortably.

His eyes wandered to her knees against his will, as if pulled by wires. He snapped them back to the road.

"Aren't you wondering why I'm being so calm about this?" she asked him. "Why I didn't call the police until I asked about the reward? It all must seem very crass and grubby."

He shrugged. "All I want is for the kidnappings to end."

"Your brother catching a lot of flak, then?"

"He can handle it." Indeed.

"There's a rumor going around," she said, "but you probably heard it before I did."

He shrugged his shoulders.

"They say it's the skinheads. All of the kidnapped girls were white. The reason the girls were released is because they'd been impregnated by the head honcho in order to form a new master race."

He looked at her. "Eleven-year-olds?"

"That's not too young sometimes."

"Sounds pretty shaky."

"There are other rumors."

"UFOs?"

"Of course *that,* and rumors like the girls' brains have been transplanted at a secret government facility."

He frowned. "Transplanted with what?"

"Nobody knows. Einstein's brain, Reagan's brain. Brains discovered in jars under the ocean, preserved for millennia by the doomed Atlanteans."

"Very thoughtful of them."

She smiled. "I've never met a man from Atlantis I didn't like."

He smiled back. "Myself, I favor the Atlantis Braves in the playoffs."

They laughed together. All of a sudden here they were, whooping it up like old pals. Darkman's heart jumped up into his throat and began pulsing there, not an altogether unpleasant sensation. But his face was the face of a grandfather, even his phony hands wore a few liver spots among the wrinkles and veins. He checked his watch and found that he had plenty of time before this awful face went the way of the Hula Hoop.

"This is the road I jog along," she said. "No muggers or kidnappers up here. The air is so clean that the stars at night barely twinkle."

"Still dangerous, though," he said.

"So is taking a bus."

He had to nod. So was lab work. Look where it had landed *him*. He drove on without thinking much, enjoying the woodland scenery and the few houses that came into view between the trees on the hilltops. Hard to imagine a body up here.

"So," she said, "I know your last name. What's in front of it?"

He deliberated quickly. What exactly *was* his first name? What went well with Goodrow? Mortimer Goodrow? No way. Fred Goodrow? Uck. There was another name in the back of his thoughts . . . Percy. Hell no, that was the dead guy.

She reached out and touched his arm. "Did you forget your own name?"

He snapped his head around to look at her. "Gilligan," he said promptly, then died inside. Of all the stupid, numbskull names to—

"Like in the old TV show?"

He grinned lamely while imaginary sweat flooded down his face, which should have been flaming red about now. "Yeah. Gilligan Goodrow." He felt his dignity dive into his shoes and start tearing at the stitching, needing to find somebody else to live with.

"Okay," she said, sounding playfully gruff, "as the P.I. team of Gilligan Goodrow and Darla Dalton, Limited and Incorporated, we shall examine the body. Take a left at this gravel road."

He did, relieved that she had not laughed at him, feeling absurdly proud of the nice new car he was driving. But wait a minute. What right did he have to enjoy any of this? Julie's niece was God-knew-where, a man was dead of multiple stabbings, two little girls were locked in a psych ward, he had no face and was a fraud and a murderer and was very likely insane, his former girlfriend was falling for a total stranger, and he was driving a stolen car.

You talk about having a bad day.

"Stop here," Darla said, and he did. He shut off the engine.

She opened her door. "This way."

He got out and followed her, trying to concentrate on the task at hand, which was not only to check the body for anything pertinent, but to determine how it had wound up here. If the man had dragged himself some distance after being stabbed, there might be a trail to follow. But if he'd been dumped out of a car, he might as well be on the moon. And there was one other item he wanted to check. If he found what he thought he might, it would mean that Shawna was dead.

Darla slowed, and Darkman hurried to her side. She pointed. "Down here in that little gully."

They went on. From a distance he could see a patch of white on the ground ahead. When they got closer he saw that it was a shirt.

They drew up beside the body. Darkman had to study the bright sky for a moment to settle his stomach. The young man, as promised, was about twenty. His stomach was a mess, and pieces of his insides were scattered behind him, forming a trail of bloody entrails. It was obvious he had crawled some distance; the path behind him was a shallow trench.

Darkman squatted and took off the man's shoes and socks, thinking they might have been replaced on his feet for some reason.

He examined his toes.

No burns. No traces of wax.

No ritual murder, then. Maybe. And Shawna might still be alive, not sacrificed by some horrible cult. She would have endured unspeakable torture, perhaps, but she would be alive. Maybe.

"Gilligan," Darla said softly, "I won't even ask what you're doing."

Darkman stood. "I think this whole ugly kidnapping business is the work of a religious cult. Quasi-religious, anyway. Devil-worshipers or the like."

"That's scary," she said, and looked around. A cool breeze was moving gently through the trees. It was too nice a day, Darkman thought, to have to look at a body like this. The man's face was awful, his mouth wrenched open, his eyes bulging as if he had gaped into the cavern of hell. Maybe he had. But if he was involved in this cult, how did he fit into the rituals? The cult tortured young girls, not wiry young men covered with tattoos. Unless, maybe, the tattooed guy lying here was a traitor or an informant who had to be silenced.

He could spend all afternoon guessing and still not be right. He turned to Darla, who was staring at the body as mystified as if examining an unsolved Rubik's Cube. "I'm going to follow his trail," Darkman told her. "You can wait in the car if you'd like. The keys are in it, if you want to listen to the radio."

She looked up at him, so pretty and so likable. Again he wondered what strange malady she had inflicted on him. A terrible thought struck him. Was this lust another side effect of the Rangeveritz operation? His emotions were wild, often impossible to control. And now his baser urges were surfacing. Where would this new affliction lead him? Would he fall madly in love with every pretty face for no good reason? Or would it lead him even farther?

They walked back to the car. "There's some kind of goop all over the dashboard," she said, and he was glad to give up on further speculation. "And what's all that yellow dust on the floor?"

He only had to think for a second. "I spilled my fingerprint kit." This was an extraordinarily good lie on such short notice, in his opinion. "Be back soon," he said, and walked away before she could see his thoughts in his eyes.

A minute later, trudging up the slope out of sight of the car, he heard the radio go on. It seemed, when she found a station and stuck with it, that Darla was fond of rock oldies, just as he was. Dire Straits sang a ballad about the Sultans of Swing.

He walked on, and the music slowly faded as he wondered what he might find and what he would do with it. For the first time since the explosion he wished he owned a gun—for use against the cult, if he found it, and for use against another terrible evil, if his mind continued to deteriorate.

He would use it to stop himself before someone else had to.

CHAPTER

20

Last-minute Preparations

The faithful had begun to arrive at Hopewell's mansion. The early birds were the hardest drinkers, and they were excited at the idea of celebrating again so soon after the last memorable gathering. Most of them were core members who had been with Hopewell from the start, back in the chicken-sacrificing days, when the smell of burning feathers used to make them both sick and younger, thanks to Hopewell's convoluted teachings. He knew that if he had not found them, they would have joined some other outlandish group, anything to distract them from the knowledge that they were very old and very rich but still too poor to buy back their youth.

Hopewell was nervously pacing the hallway at the head of the stairs, checking his watch again and again, at times stalking to a window to hurl the curtains aside and peer out. His driveway was a winding ribbon of asphalt bordered by stately square-cut hedges, his front lawn a massive stretch of perfect grass surrounded by woods. The lawn mower, a big yellow John Deere, sat forlornly where the groundskeeper had left it after Fritz fired him for cutting the lawn too early. Now it seemed like a silly complaint. He wondered if all this drinking was affecting his mind; even now, this early, he had a glass of luke-warm Jack Daniel's in one hand and the intent in his mind to refill it when it was empty.

Fritz had been gone an awfully long time. Supposedly he was returning the U-Haul and getting his car back. The shotguns were stacked helter-skelter on the living room sofas and chairs. If he did not return, Hopewell would have to conduct the class on how to load and fire the weapons, and he wasn't all that sure how to handle them. He was a preacher, not a gunslinger. And what if Fritz had caught a flight to some safe place and was gone for good? He was the working partner, and Hopewell could hardly replace him by running a Help Wanted ad in the local paper. Even worse, what if Fritz was down at police headquarters copping a plea, telling the cops everything? Please, no. Anything but that.

Down the hall he heard Shawna Hastings moan. She had been moaning a lot as the day wore on. He wondered idly if she was hungry, although it hardly mattered. She would be officially defiled soon and dumped off some-where. The memory of his love for her was already old and tarnished. She had almost robbed him of something precious. With her beauty and her maiden charm she had almost robbed Norman Hopewell of his self-respect. For that, and her tendency to scream when he was hung over, she would be defiled tonight and hauled away by that remaining goon, Pocketknife, if he showed up. Hopewell was getting very tired of incompetent and unreliable people.

He checked his watch again, then watched his devoted followers as they laughed and scoured the place for whiskey. It was Fritz's job to go to the liquor store and provide tonight's refreshments. With nothing to drink, these alcoholics might accidentally sober up and realize how bizarre this whole cult was.

Shawna moaned again. He hustled angrily down the hall into the bedroom. *"Shut the hell up!"* he hissed at her. He made a motion to hit her, then stopped himself.

He had already beaten her half silly. She was out of her mind now, semiconscious, moaning with delirium. He hoped she would snap out of it when the defilement began; the flock would enjoy hearing her scream as her youth was channeled into their bodies. Man, did they love that.

He strode to the window again, flung the heavy curtains aside, and saw with great relief that Fritz was driving up. He hadn't run away after all; he was still a reliable partner. Hopewell put his glass on a table and hurried downstairs and outside, ignoring his followers' complaints about the dearth of booze.

Outside, Fritz was climbing out of his Chrysler, checking his watch, and barking out an excuse. "Do you have any idea," he snapped before Hopewell could say a word, "how long it takes to transport ninety-five bottles of liquor from a store into this car? Don't even start on me, Norm, just give me a hand."

"The place is still a shambles from last night," Hopewell said. "I thought you were going to clean it up. And how come the damned lawn mower is still sitting in the yard?"

Fritz planted his hands on his hips. "Christ, Norm! Do this. Do that. Do this. Who died and made you Hitler? And have you noticed lately that I do all the work around here while you sit on your ass? Once a month you flap your jaws and do your little act, and the rest of the time I do everything else."

Hopewell ignored him. "What about the delivery boy, that Pocketknife kid? Did you get ahold of him?"

Fritz jammed his fat face closer. "I don't even know his last name, Norm! Am I supposed to divine a phone number?"

Hopewell noticed at the corner of his sight that a few of his old and thirsty followers had come outside and were watching their guru being browbeaten by his number one disciple. He felt like telling them to go find a nursing home to die in. Instead he said, "Have no fear, my children! The wine of youth will flow tonight!"

They smiled. One doddering old man clapped. Hopewell turned back to Fritz with a serene smile. "Looks like you'll have to dump the girl yourself, then," he growled too softly for them to hear.

Fritz scowled, but kept his voice low as well. "It's too damned dangerous. She's seen your face and mine, since you decided you had to gaze into her baby blues. Let's just sacrifice her and get it over with."

Hopewell thought about it. Sacrifice his bride? Well, he considered himself divorced now. She was all bruised and disheveled and frankly, she looked terrible. "Fine," he said. "I'll need a knife."

Fritz offered him a thin, contemptuous smile. "Think you could manage to find one yourself?"

Hopewell snorted. "Let's just haul the booze in, you and me."

"Forget it," Fritz said, watching as a gray Mercedes appeared at the head of the driveway. "I'll ask one of the flock to hand the faithful a couple of bottles as they arrive. Sort of like a smorgasbord."

Hopewell nodded, satisfied. He went inside with Fritz on his heels. Immediately he heard the girl moan; she sounded like a baby fawn in pain.

Fritz looked at him darkly. "Have you been worshiping her again?"

"Haven't touched her," Hopewell lied. "I think she's flipping out." He looked at his watch. "I feel like speeding things up. My nerves can't take much more of her."

"The ceremony has to be held at midnight," Fritz growled. "Your own rules."

"Screw the rules. As soon as everybody's here we'll start the defilement."

"You've gotta admit the ritual is pretty damned revolting. What if they're not drunk enough?"

"Just make sure they are," Hopewell sighed.

Fritz checked his watch. "I'll go check and see how the flock is doing." He hurried away. At the door he stopped long enough to cast Hopewell a weary look. His eyes took in the mansion, which looked as if it had been devastated by a large bomb. Bottles and empty snack bags were everywhere, and cigarette burns peppered the carpet. One of the chandeliers was askew; perhaps it would fall and squash some old pervert. Already somebody was cranking up the massive stereo system, spilling the brain-numbing sound of the B-52s throughout the room. Fritz shook his aching head and stepped outside.

Just a few more hours and he would be away from this lunatic asylum forever.

CHAPTER

21

Doubts upon Doubts

Darkman had lost the trail. There was not a drop of Indian blood in his veins. No known relative had been a pathfinder or tracker or sleuth. His family tree contained not one Eagle Scout. Darkman himself had never advanced beyond the rank of Tenderfoot because he did not like the outdoors all that much, and camping not at all. In addition, his scoutmaster had fancied himself to be General Patton and had taken great delight in enforcing military discipline on ten-year-old Peyton Westlake and his bewildered companions. For these reasons Darkman was now convinced he was a failed woodsman walking in circles.

The trouble had started at a small ditch that was either a minuscule creek or a long puddle. The dead man's scooped-out trail vanished there. Was this, then, where the cult had dumped him? If so, where were *their* tracks? To him the track of a raccoon looked much like the track of a deer, and he could find neither here. Everything looked as if it had been walked upon. And everything looked undisturbed, too. He squatted and picked up a leaf that was lying at the water's edge. Was there a smear of dry blood on it or was that just a natural streak in the leaf? Fall might be coming early this year, so he didn't know which. He wondered if Darla Dalton, his partner in this enterprise, was any better at tracking.

Probably not. There wasn't much need for trackers anymore. Bloodhounds were more reliable.

He looked back to check his path from the car to here. The ruts made by the man's elbows and dragging feet were still clear enough to see, though the woods were getting denser and blocking much of the afternoon sunlight. Unfortunately the breeze was growing stronger, already trying to cover the track with a fresh drift of leaves. This search was as good as hopeless.

But he didn't want to turn back. This lead was almost as good as the last one had been, he felt sure of it. "Mensa material." It couldn't be coincidence.

He shuffled around and looked up the slope. There was nothing unusual to see among the maples and oaks and catalpas with their long cigar-shaped seed pods. A choppy clump of briers looked somewhat bent and broken, so he walked to it. By purposely unfocusing his eyes he thought he could see a zigzag line on the ground beyond it, angling upward. Maybe the guy had lost control and rolled down this way. Well, it was the only thing he had to go on. He just hoped that when the search teams set out to look for *him,* they would bring some experts along.

On he went while time passed and the shadows grew longer. He was making more stops than progress, and he was becoming seriously worried about getting lost. This area was wilder than before. At one point he saw a fox, or a dog of some sort, but it took one look at him and fled. He touched his face. It was still there; he had not frightened the animal that way. He began to worry that his face would disintegrate while he was driving Darla home. She was witty and bright, but would she be able to handle the transformation? He doubted it. Even Julie had nearly fainted when she laid eyes on his naked skull for the first time. If he hoped to worm himself into Darla's life, he'd better be careful.

What are you thinking, old pal?

He had been wondering about his motives. He had purposely stayed out of Julie's life because she did not deserve to have a freak for a lover. Why burden another woman with his problems, which went far deeper than looks?

Do you still love Julie?

He stopped examining the ground, stopped walking. The breeze flapped his tie slightly, tossed some of his nylon hair about. Did he still love her? That was a fine question. Did she still love him? Another fine one.

He had to face the truth: he and Julie were growing apart. He had done his job well. She had a boyfriend who was handsome and rich. Darkman had his rats and his spiders and his computers and his loneliness. Wasn't that what he had wanted? Or was he just immersed in self-pity? Hadn't he really wanted Julie to pine away for him, to grow old with a candle in the window, waiting for his return? That sounded romantic. It sounded like a nobly tragic life for both of them. But as he had read in one of the Peanuts comic strips, a tragic life was romantic only if it happened to somebody else. In reality a tragic life was misery for the participants. So why had he tried to romanticize his plight?

It was a valid question. For the better part of the last two years he had resigned himself to the idea of spending the rest of his life like Alexandre Dumas's Man in the Iron Mask, cast out of society with no hope of returning. Tragic, romantic misery. Toss in Julie, and you have a pair of star-crossed lovers à la Romeo and Juliet. Yet he had never thought Julie would find someone else. Her life was supposed to be as heartbreakingly tragic as his, but somewhere along the line she had been handed the wrong script. She was seeking now her own happiness. So where did that leave him? To phrase it better, where had he left himself?

Lost in the middle of the woods, that's where. He wondered darkly if he was on a one-man hunt for

Shawna just so he could present her to Julie and say "See how great I am? Now forget your new boyfriend and go back to burning a candle in the window."

Maybe it was true. And even if it wasn't, Julie had endured so much over the past two years that their relationship was probably dead and buried anyway.

Which left him free to pursue the beguiling Darla Dalton and turn her life upside down as well. Unless, of course, he was really going off the deep end and would just wind up raping and murdering her.

He clutched his head in his hands. These doubts were torturing him. As a researcher he had been trained to question things. As Darkman the questions were driving him insane.

And as if for the final course of this horrible mental meal, his mind created a swift, fleeting picture of Darla Dalton slashed and bleeding to death in a red Cadillac with her dress in rags, Darkman standing to one side wearing an insane leer, panting and drooling.

He tilted his face to the sky. *"Nooooooo!"* he screamed to the branches overhead and the clouds gathering above them. As if in answer, the wind kicked up and set about erasing the trail even more.

CHAPTER

22

The Gathering Storm

The party got started as soon as the last member was carted from his home by the two other members Hopewell had sent to find him. He was a crotchety old fellow whose name Hopewell couldn't remember, not that it mattered. It was the numbers that counted, and after three head counts the number was finally forty-two.

The member of the flock who had been outside handing out the liquor came in and locked the door, the remaining bottles clutched in his arms. Fritz was busy presenting a shotgun and ten shells to each person. Hopewell, standing at the head of the stairs hidden in shadow, heard them ooh and aah and giggle with excitement. One man complained good-naturedly that he was still so hung over from last time that he could barely imagine another ceremony tonight, but by the god of youth, he was glad for it. Hopewell was relieved and gladdened by such tidings. One wheezing old grandpa boasted that he felt ten years younger each time they had one of these holy hoedowns, and Hopewell had to suppress the urge to laugh out loud. Too much was at stake here for laughter. Tonight was the Ceremony of Youthful Unity.

163

They wandered about, these aged rich, in Norman Hopewell's party-ruined mansion, wondering at the weight of their new weapons and expressing their delight at how well-oiled and shiny they were. Metal clicked against metal as they fumbled with their new toys, pumping the chambers open, dry-firing the triggers. Hopewell discovered suddenly that he really did love these people in a distant, fatherly way, these tired old buffoons who had lost their faith in reality and transferred it to him instead. With a little of Fritz's training they would become an armed militia to guard not against any outside enemy, though he would soon tell them that, but against potential traitors among their own ranks.

He flipped on the light at the upstairs landing and stepped into view. For this special occasion he had put on his flaming red robe and applied enough makeup around his eyes to make them look huge and mysterious under the shadow of his hood. He raised his arms for silence.

Forty-two faces turned to look up at him. Somebody turned off the stereo. Quiet fell like a dark shroud.

"My children," he murmured gravely.

He let the silence stretch out for a long moment. Outside, a hint of thunder rumbled in the west, promising early darkness and some added drama for tonight's ceremony.

He could feel his mind shifting gears, an automatic response to the seriousness of his coming message and to the faces that were staring up at him. He was very sure of his persuasive talent, but he had no idea, aside from his limited training, why he had been given this gift that he used so nobly. It was his firm conviction that, given enough time, he could sell food stamps to a Rockefeller. These people here, before they became involved with him, had probably been ordinary old men and women, but he had tapped their own darkest fears and found the hidden need in each of them.

Was that so awful? Thousands made the yearly trek to Lourdes in France, hoping to be saved from death by the healing waters. Rich people by the hundreds journeyed to Mexican cancer clinics to be fed apricot pits. Psychic surgeons in the Philippines extracted chicken guts from false thumb tips and claimed they were removing tumors, and people spent millions to consult them. Hopewell's own therapy was no more hokey than any other. These people were terrified of death, and he was relieving their terror with false remedies. And who could know for sure? A person who believed he was immune to death might just live a long, long time by the sheer power of positive thinking.

So in a way, he reasoned, this was not a cult of dangerous fools; it was a cult of terrified fools. The defiling of the virgins was a damn sight more humane than the things they *could* have been doing. And as for human sacrifice, if it made his people live longer, the loss of life was justifiable.

Having talked himself into it once again, a victim of his own powers of persuasion, he lowered his arms and contorted his face into something properly Hitlerian. "A devil has arisen to destroy us," he blared. "Tonight, my brethren, we will learn to fight. Mr. Fritz will teach you how to use these mighty weapons. As he works among you, I will explain how we shall defeat those who could deprive us of our youth. We must unite more strongly than ever before. Tonight is the Ceremony of Youthful Unity!"

They cheered and waved their shotguns and bottles overhead. The scene reminded Hopewell of a wartime photo of victorious GIs—but with fifty years added to their faces. The ages didn't matter. It did not, he assured himself, take much strength to pull a trigger.

And now it was simply a matter of turning his rhetoric up to full volume, which he could do with the ease that came from many years of practice.

As the grand guru ranted and foamed at the top of the stairs, Fritz found himself staring up at him in rapt wonder, forgetting his duties for a few moments, then coming to himself and moving on to show the next doddering idiot how to load and fire his new popgun. He practically had to scream in their faces to get their attention. Somewhere along the line he had pulled a bottle of Bacardi rum out of one stupefied woman's hand and made it his own. The liquor helped the faithful receive the message of truth; it helped Fritz stay on the right track—to end this night and go shopping for some sunblock and a Portuguese dictionary at an airport gift shop.

Thunder drummed outside again, closer this time. On the car radio he had heard that a major storm was moving in from the west. Now he mentally added some Dramamine to his shopping list; it could be a bouncy flight and he did not intend to be sick all over the only set of clothes he would have, having left all his belongings behind—a small price to pay for escaping this mad enterprise in one piece. He deemed it highly possible that he might pick up a murder-for-hire job or two among the Rio tourists. That would pay him enough to set himself up in style when Hopewell's money ran out. As usual he had appointed one of the women to pass the collection plate. As soon as she had given it back to him he'd tucked all the cash into the back of his underwear.

He pushed his way through the crowd after a while, tired of explaining the same things over and over, and paused by the sliding glass patio doors to look outside. Clouds blocked the sun totally now. Little dust devils were kicking up on the tennis court's surface; scattering leaves were collecting against the statues. As he watched, a jagged streak of lightning touched down in the surrounding woods. Seconds later the sky was rocked by a huge crash.

He sighed to himself, lifted his bottle, and took a long drink, wondering. How had he and Hopewell gotten away with this for so long? And for that matter, how had it devolved from a simple band of old folks and their spiritual leader dancing and praying for endless youth to forty-two people carrying guns? How had it changed from chickens ritualistically bled into earthen pots to little girls stripped naked for these human demons to fondle and abuse? And then, of course, there was that awful, mind-bending murder. But it had been necessary, because Fritz needed money to survive. Everybody did.

He had long ago ceased to fret about where the cash came from. Killing Hopewell's pretty young wife had not been the first murder he'd committed for money. During his most desperate financial crisis Fritz had personally placed a small nail underneath his daughter's saddle, back down on the ranch in Oklahoma many years ago. The horse had bucked her off on schedule, but she had landed in grass instead of on the rocks he had ridden into with her. Sweating and shaking, he had found it necessary to bludgeon her to death with a rock. Her life insurance, after the brief investigation, had been a check for sixty thousand dollars. He no longer woke up screaming. He no longer dreamed about it at all.

He did not understand why these old people wanted to live forever. In his own forty-six years he had already become tired of life. Perhaps in Rio he would settle down for good, take up painting or sculpture. His daughter's name had been Cindy. That thought had not come to him in ages.

He looked once more into the dismal sky, feeling that same bleakness seep into his soul. He straightened with a startled jerk.

He growled at the sky and went back to do his job.

CHAPTER

23

Pieces Falling into Place

The rain started to patter down when Darkman was near the crest of the mountain. Peyton Westlake had spent some time in Wyoming and Colorado on separate sabbaticals from the university. Both were very mountainous states, so to think of this glorified hill as a mountain was a wild stretch for his imagination, although the locals believed that if it slanted up for more than ten yards, it had to be a mountain. But, mountain or hill, he was at the top where the woods had been thinned, and he was still on the verge of being lost.

From this vantage point he could see the other crests, quite far away indeed. And through the greenery and the mist of rain he also saw a smattering of huge houses, winding driveways, even an electrical tower of some sort thrusting up between the hills like a giant Erector set construction supporting wires. It would be impossible to get so far away from civilization here that you could stay lost for long. However, Darkman had no desire to hike downward again and wind up going in circles all night. He would go to the nearest house and use the telephone. But . . . whom to call?

The man from Indiana had not been nice enough to have a cellular phone in his Cadillac. That rejected the idea of somehow calling Darla Dalton. He could call Julie and ask her for a ride, but too many doubts still cluttered his mind to see her face-to-face again. In the end, he supposed, he would have to call a cab.

And too bad he hadn't brought an umbrella. It looked like the weather forecast was right on the money for this gloomy afternoon.

He pushed through a clump of brush, picking up a few burrs on his socks, and saw a tennis court. Beyond it was a huge, slightly unmanicured lawn dotted with concrete statues of dragons and other mythological beasts. Far to the right was a putting green, its colorful flagstick waving and slapping in the growing wind. Whoever lived here, he felt sure, did not receive a welfare check every two weeks. Through the patio doors he could see a short plump man staring out at the sky. After a moment the man turned suddenly and ambled away. Inside the house, too, Darkman could hear someone speaking loudly, maybe even making a speech, by the sound of it. Could be a small political rally, he thought indifferently. Could also be an auction to peddle the family heirlooms. Would they mind letting him use their phone?

He touched his face. It was wet from the rain but still firm. The dimness of the woods and the absence of sunlight were lengthening its life, which on a graph was a straight line that suddenly plunged downward with all the grace of a falling brick. He had once vowed not to reappear in society until the skin was permanent, but it now seemed that that would never happen. Which meant rebuilding his life around these new limitations.

More fodder for the mental mill. But standing in knee-high weeds in a driving rain was no time to digest it. He started forward, hoping that the homeowner did not have roving Doberman pinschers or pit bulls on duty, or have a security system that would get him into trouble. He just wanted to rap on the back door, ask the butler for the phone, and wait around front for his cab. Find Darla again, drive her home, and start writing secret-admirer letters. For fun he could design a face so handsome as to make Robert Redford look like a reject from the ugly farm.

He admired the statues as he passed, fancied himself on the tennis court exchanging lobs with Darla and lounging by the pool—there had to be one around this place somewhere—while lighting a cigar with a thousand-dollar bill.

You don't even smoke.

He could learn. With enough money, he could learn a lot. He stopped at the door and peeked uneasily through the glass, feeling like an intruder. It would probably make sense to hike around front and ring the door chime.

He saw something then that sent a jolt of horror careening through his veins.

A man was flapping his arms at the top of a long, winding staircase. Flashy diamond rings sparkled on his fingers. His face was shadowed by a floppy hood attached to a scarlet monk's robe.

A roomful of people watched him in obvious awe. They carried bottles of liquor and rifles. Or shotguns, maybe.

He ducked out of sight and pressed his back against the side of the house, his mouth suddenly dry, his breath whistling in his throat. He had found the cult. That, or a very early Halloween party. He dared to peek back in for a moment. They seemed to be men, most of them. Old men.

Old men? What was a houseful of nice old men doing slugging down liquor by the bottle? Why the guns? What was with the guy in the robe spouting his indecipherable message?

He decided not to wonder. Cults, all cults, were populated by weirdos. There was a very fine line between established religions and off-the-wall religions. Snake handlers read out of the same Bible as Mormon polygamists. It did not matter if these old folks worshiped

Buddha or banana peels; they were hurting people in the process. They had to be stopped.

His first thought was to run for help. But the nearest house was at least a mile away, probably more, and this dismal day was trying very hard now to become a dismal night. There might be a car out front he could steal, but he had not studied hot-wiring in college. At the slightest hint that they were discovered, these people would scatter like rabbits, so he had to move very carefully.

One man against a houseful—pretty dismal odds, especially since he didn't have so much as a slingshot.

It occurred to him to leave immediately. He knew where the house was, roughly, and he could bring the police here later, maybe tomorrow. A whole SWAT team.

But what if a little girl was in there, about to be offered up to the gods? It could even be Shawna.

That thought pushed him into action.

He moved away from the wall and was about to dart around front when the patio door slid open and a wispy-haired old man poked his head outside. He looked as if he was in the last stages of a terrible disease. As Darkman watched, unseen, the old guy retched and a stream of vomit left his mouth to splatter on the cement and Darkman's shoes. When he was done he swiveled his head, fastened his bleary eyes on Darkman, and frowned.

"Who the hell are you?" he demanded.

Darkman felt a little sick himself.

Darla Dalton, bored and vaguely worried, turned the radio off. The nice old gent, the police chief's brother Gilligan, had certainly been gone a long time. She wasn't particularly worried about him, but sitting here with a dead, practically dismembered body lying not far away was becoming spooky, especially since the sun had been obliterated by the clouds and the wind had picked up, not to mention the rain, the thunder, and the bright flashes of lightning that occasionally exploded in the sky.

When she had found the body in these woods today,

she had not been jogging as she'd told Gilligan, but that was another matter. Jogging or not, the man's ghoulish scream had just about stalled her heart; finding him had just about emptied her stomach. But she had remained, all in all, cool.

She felt guilty for having waited so long to report the body, but priorities were priorities. She needed money, needed it fast, no matter how she had to get it. She had to admit she was being damned mercenary, but she desperately hoped to get the reward money. Now that hope was as good as gone; this tattooed corpse had nothing to do with the kidnapped girls.

In reality she had not known much about the rash of kidnappings. Her own problems had kept her away from the newspapers, rendering her unable to concentrate, but the big reward ad had jumped right out at her, and she'd had a feeling this morning while trying to choke down breakfast, a false feeling based on desperation, that it was somehow providential. Yet she did believe in fate, and the possibility still existed that fate had had a hand in her finding the body and contacting this nice old man. Call her recklessly optimistic, but if she played her cards right, Gilligan Goodrow could be her salvation. She knew for a fact that he had at least fifty thousand dollars to part with.

Rain drummed on the roof and splattered on the windshield. She reached up and bent the rearview mirror down to see herself. She already knew she was pretty, had been told it a million times by every hopeful man she'd ever met, but she was deteriorating fast. Crow's feet were appearing at the corners of her eyes and laugh lines were developing at the corners of her mouth. She was surprised not to see a single gray hair among the dark ones, but she was of Basque lineage and the Basques had a tendency to age gracefully, at least in the old country. Her greatest enemy was the sun, which was mercilessly hard on her pale skin, and she had to avoid it.

She was also not Darla. Where that name had come

from she did not know. But she had been reduced to lying a lot lately.

She decided she would take advantage of the old—or at least middle-aged—gent who was being so kind. She was not, by nature, a conniving woman, but she was a survivor. Gilligan could afford to be parted from his thousands; she could not afford to be parted from her freedom.

So she waited, tense with nervousness, constantly flicking the radio on then off, going quietly mad. If she handled herself right she could wrap Gilligan around her little finger tighter than the stripes on a barber pole, and then she could get at his money. The day might come when she could apologize and repay him.

She felt that if he knew the truth, he would not hate her. So why not tell him the truth now?

Because too much was at stake. He could laugh in her face. He could tell her to go to the cops or get heroically involved and *really* foul things up. All she needed was his money, and she estimated that she had about twenty-four hours left to get it. Prior to this she had been working on her best friend's boyfriend, and he had been forking over little sums now and then, just enough to unwittingly buy time for her, but he was not made of money, and now he was getting pushy. He was hinting very crudely at some sack time. This she could not do to her friend. But if this Gilligan got stubborn or wanted to know too many details, or if he demanded something in return, could she give in to him? Would she?

She decided that she would. She would even marry him for that money. She had to be hard now, as hard as nails, willing to do anything short of murder to bring an end to this extended nightmare. She would do what had to be done.

But Gilligan was not back yet, had been gone far too long. It struck her belatedly that his brand-new car must have cost forty thousand dollars, and although that was not quite enough to clear her, it sure was a hell of a lot better than what she had now, which was zip.

She put her hand on the keys. Hanging from the chain was a plastic disk that proclaimed Gilligan was a Taurus. The reverse side announced that his name was Burt.

Burt?

She shrugged to herself. Burt was a damn sight more believable than Gilligan. Was he lying to her, or did the car and key chain belong to one of his kids? She popped the glove box open. It was stuffed full of blank business forms, addressed envelopes, and business cards bound by a rubber band. She worked one free and read it. "Burton J. Dougherty," it said. "Licensed Real Estate Appraiser, Commercial Properties a Specialty." This was followed by phone and fax numbers.

A little sigh of dismay escaped her. This all looked very suspicious. The floor on the passenger side was littered with fast-food bags and empty pop cans she hadn't noticed before. One bag proclaimed that Super Torero Tacos were the best taste of Mexico that Illinois had to offer. Highly suspicious. And how could she sell a hot car, or even a cold one, without some kind of title? She checked the glove compartment again, but nobody was *that* stupid.

Now she felt a little angry. She had one day left. Instead of doing something about it, she was sitting in a stolen car in the middle of the woods waiting for a lying old geezer to stagger out of the woods and hand her a fortune.

Enough of this nonsense. She started the car and peeled out in a spray of mud and leaves, saying to hell with it all.

CHAPTER

24

Nice Place You Got

I had to get some air," Darkman panted. "I was feeling really sick. Kind of like you just were."

The old guy bobbed his head. "Sometimes I get really sick without much warning, and then I'm fine." He hiccuped, then swallowed with a grimace. "I love these meetings, but at my age I gotta slow down once in a while." He ruefully eyed the puddle he had made on the cement. "If I'm getting younger, somebody ought to tell my stomach." Now he looked at Darkman again. "You new here?"

"Yes," Darkman said, still panting. He might be impervious to external pain, but he was not impervious to scares and heart attacks. Getting caught at the back door had just about turned his wig white. And what the hell was this getting-younger business? "I just joined up."

"New members are usually formally introduced to the group. But maybe Brother Hopewell has changed the policy, now that we're getting so many new people. Who sponsored you?"

Darkman stared at him. "Joe," he said. "Joe sponsored me."

"Well, I'll tell you what." He stepped fully out and slid the door shut. Under the protection of the eaves he propped his shotgun against the house and took a quick slug out of his bottle. "I've known Joe for quite a while now, and when I first met him I would have told you he had about two days to live, but look at him now! He can jump around like a chicken. The ceremonies don't seem to work as well for me, but I do feel a damn sight younger sometimes. Check this out." He rolled up the right sleeve of his shirt and flexed his biceps. "Tell me an old man can't keep up with the young bucks."

Darkman admired his muscle. "Looks like progress."

The old guy grinned. "The calendar says I'm seventy-two. My body tells me I'm about sixty." His grin faltered. "Say, didn't you get a gun yet? I thought everybody—"

Darkman silenced him by driving his fist hard against the old man's Adam's apple in a sudden thrust. He thudded against the house and slid rapidly to a sitting position, then slumped over as a thin line of blood seeped between his slightly parted lips.

Darkman snatched up his rifle and worked the bottle out of his hand. Whether he was dead or not, he neither knew nor cared. Putting the gun and the bottle—some cheap brand of whiskey—aside, Darkman dragged him around to the side of the house where he was less likely to be seen. He hustled back, trying to stay under the eaves, which struck him as absurd since he was already soaked. He scurried back again, hurriedly traded coats with the old man, then went back again and slid the door open a cautious crack to look inside. No one had heard the old man thump against the wall, apparently. Taking a preparatory gulp of air he slid the door farther open and stepped inside, putting on the same foppish grin that the others seemed to be wearing as they listened to the man—Brother Hopewell?—rant at the top of the stairs.

All the curtains had been drawn, and the light inside was sufficiently dim for him to blend in. Fortunately, if the old man had been correct, there were a lot of new recruits here. He only hoped no one would recognize him as the chief of police. *That* would be hard to explain. It was also lucky that he was dressed in a business suit. Most of the old folks here were wearing either a suit or slacks and a sweater. Yet insane cultists or not, the people here were obviously not street bums. The smell of money was almost as thick in the air as the smell of cigars often smoked and whiskey often spilled. Over it all hung the aroma of stale vomit.

He eyed the great guru and saw only a lackluster gent in an absurd red robe that exposed his Gucci shoes and a hint of white socks. Currently he was going on about external enemies hell-bent on the destruction of "his children," along with pleas and demands for greater unity. What he had to say was really of no importance to Darkman. It sufficed that he was insane and had brought a lot of people along with him for the ride. Still Darkman could not believe the faces around him, ordinary folks except for the sheen of madness in their eyes and the shotguns in their hands. It struck him that in 1978 a madman named Jim Jones had told his nine hundred followers to poison themselves and their children, and they had done so. Unbelievable. Bodies stretching for hundreds of yards in a jungle clearing. At that moment Peyton Westlake had decided that the most dangerous man in the world was the man who could convince more than twelve others that he was on a mission from God.

He listened to the sermon restlessly for a few minutes, with rainwater draining out of his wig, the shotgun growing heavier in one hand, the whiskey getting warm in the other. There was no sign of a child bound and gagged for whatever ritual they had in mind, no man around young enough to qualify as a sacrificial lamb. Perhaps they only needed one a month. This gathering could easily be just a fund-raiser. But the guns? Brother Hopewell up there was a very hard man to figure out.

Darkman slowly eased himself away from the crowd, staying close to the wall, wanting to scout this big house for the simplest way to bring help—a telephone in a room where he could use it without getting caught. He finally was able to squeeze around a corner and strike off on his own, treading lightly, taking in the sights.

It became obvious that not many people lived here on a regular basis. Some rooms were empty and seemed to have no use at all. If the front room qualified as a living room, then the house had two more of them, chandeliers twinkling lightlessly in the mellow dimness, the mansion itself giving off an aura of disuse. There were bathrooms galore loaded with gold fixtures, marble floors, empty hot tubs, majestic sunken baths. He found a door that opened on a four-car garage that housed only one magnificent Mercedes and some lawn equipment that smelled strongly of gasoline. He needed to find a way upstairs—an elevator, a dumbwaiter, anything. While creeping down one hallway he almost blundered back into the crowd again, and hastily backtracked. All in all, this place could have housed half the population of India. The upper floor was probably equally spacious.

If he could find a way to it. He detoured through a kitchen where one nibbled-at TV dinner sat lonesomely on a large table and an immense stove was still on. He turned it off for no reason at all. On the table lay a sheet of paper with some scribbling on it. He read through it. Notes for a speech filled with hokey platitudes.

Satisfied he wouldn't find a way upstairs without passing by Brother Hopewell, he blended back into the party and suffered through some more bombastic oratory. A small fat man appeared in front of him unexpectedly and boredly asked if he knew how to use the shotgun. Darkman immediately dropped his head and mumbled an affirmative, trying to sound drunk and doing it quite well. The man moved on. He breathed again, then forced himself to take a swig of the whiskey. It was hard to be a convincing drunk without booze on his breath, he told himself as the inferior brew slid hotly into his guts. He almost gagged. If these were rich people they sure brought lousy firewater.

Hopewell was cranking up the volume even more, making Darkman hope he might just about be finished. The crowd had taken to shouting their agreement here and there and tossing amens through the air like verbal boomerangs to ricochet off the walls. They stamped their feet as Hopewell's voice slid into senseless, doglike barking and finally thundered to a stop.

Cheers rang like cannon shots. Darkman joined in the jubilation, trying only to look like a fool. Hopewell thumped down the stairs and waded into his flock, casting benedictions and waving his arms some more. Music magically thundered alive. A second later a strobe light popped weakly on, relic of the disco age, turning the crowd into a stuttering riot of colors and faces. "Dance, my children," Hopewell bellowed. "Dance and be young!"

Darkman pushed his way through the worshipers, heading for the stairway, getting slammed into by people suddenly dancing spastically. Sufficiently knocked around, breathless, he found the first step by tripping over it and falling heavily to his hands and knees. He crawled the rest of the way up, trying to look drunk and disoriented, but no one seemed to care what he looked like or where he was going. He made it to the top and scuttled away, rising only when he was safely behind a wall.

A hallway padded with thick blue carpeting stretched into the semidarkness. He edged along it, constantly turning his head back to check the stairway, and came to an open door.

Empty room.

He stepped sideways and pushed another door open. This room contained an unmade bed and a dresser that had one drawer hanging open. An empty suitcase lay open on the floor.

He went on. Empty rooms greeted his hasty inspections. One of them held a pile of smelly laundry. Another was littered with old newspapers. He could almost smell the dust lying undisturbed on windowsills and baseboards in the rest of the rooms. Finally, though, he eased a door open on a room that contained all kinds of interesting things.

A huge bed, two dressers, mirrors, big windows with the shades drawn. And on the bed, tied by her ankles and wrists, lay a naked little girl.

"Jesus," he whispered and went inside. He pulled the door carefully shut and hurried over to her. She had been bound with strips of cloth, and a rag was jammed into her mouth. She was badly bruised, bleeding a little from minor cuts, and apparently unconscious. There were teeth marks all over her face and neck, but her chest was rising and falling to the time of her breathing.

His jaw tightened with horror and anger. He discarded the gun and bottle and jerked at her restraints. The knots had been pulled into tight little balls by what had to have been a long struggle. With a brief, toneless snarl he ripped the cloth apart like paper. He left the rag in her mouth, hating it but needing to. If she made a noise it could ruin their escape.

He had no idea how to sneak out of this labyrinth of rooms and hallways without being seen. Nevertheless he ripped a sheet free from the bed and wrapped her in it. He hauled her up into his arms and tried to make her comfortable. Her head and arms dangled lifelessly.

He turned and was able to get a hand on the knob and work the door open with a foot. There he paused, beginning to breathe heavily, fighting the rage that was trying very hard to block his sense of reason. Mission number one, he ordered himself, was Shawna's rescue. Then he could come back and . . . and . . .

And what? Rip some heads off?

Yes, dammit, exactly that. And more.

He started out and nearly collided with the fat man, who was hurrying down the hall. They pedaled to a stop and looked at each other.

The fat man was toting a shotgun. He swung it up in a swift motion and got his finger on the trigger.

"What are you doing with her?" he growled, pumping

a round into the chamber. "Who gave you permission to come up here?"

Darkman stared at him while his mind went blank save for a large, seething area that was colored a bright and vivid red, the red of his hate, the red of his rage, which was slipping quickly, inexorably out of control.

CHAPTER

25

You Will Not Meet a Tall, Dark Stranger

She wasn't speeding, and there weren't any speed-limit signs, but a cop nevertheless roared up behind her in his white and blue patrol car and turned on his flashing lights. The woman who was not really named Darla Dalton pounded her fists on the Cadillac's cheerful red steering wheel. Why her? Why now? She needed time and was being delayed by an overeager mountie who wanted to fill his quota of tickets.

She thought about making a run for it. She thought about bringing the car to a screeching halt and hightailing it into the woods on foot. She thought about a lot of things, but in the end she simply pulled over onto the gravel shoulder and waited for fate and the cop to take charge while her windshield wipers slapped out a monotonous beat. The situation was out of her hands.

He took his own sweet time, doing whatever cops did before they trundled over with the bad news. Finally he got out, adjusted his hat, and smoothed his rain jacket, then joined her. Darla turned off the engine; this could take a while.

"Good evening," he said amicably, stooping a little to

look through the window as she opened it. "May I see your operator's license?"

He could have, if she'd brought it with her, but the only things she had brought from her little rental house were the clothes on her body and the glasses on her nose. Time, maybe, to slather on the charm, go into her poor-little-me act. It had never worked before, but what the heck? She slipped her glasses off and batted her eyelashes. "Mercy," she said, feigning distress, "I must have left my purse at home."

"Do tell," he said. "May I see your registration please?"

She opened the glove compartment. Business forms slipped out in a cascade. She found what looked like something a motor vehicles bureau might have printed. She handed it over, but there was no hand to hand it to. She looked over his way and they were practically nose-to-nose. He seemed to be eyeballing the goopy stuff all over the stereo knobs, and the yellow dust some of it had turned into. But so what? Was it a crime to have a goopy radio?

"You sit tight," he ordered as he snatched the registration out of her fingers and strode back to his car. She put her glasses back on and in the mirror saw him get inside his cruiser. She knew that she was very likely driving a stolen car. Again, so what? *She* hadn't stolen it; she'd just . . . borrowed it from the real thief, who was lost in the woods while impersonating the police chief's brother, having driven her here to find the body of a stranger who had been murdered by a cult of kidnappers.

Hmmm. She remembered that she had forgotten to read her horoscope today. Even Jeane Dixon couldn't have predicted a mess like this.

Once again she considered making a cannonball run. Could she rocket down the road, catch the freeway, and try to make it up north to Canada? Yeah, right. Her first stop would be the state penitentiary, then Alcatraz, reopened for her and her alone. Solitary on the Rock. Hard labor. The electric chair.

And so she waited while the policeman talked on his radio and discovered all kinds of dark secrets from the crime computers. Right on schedule he hurried back and ordered her out of the car—not at gunpoint, but close to it. He wasn't shy about frisking her, and he wasn't too nice a guy to handcuff a defenseless woman. He took the keys out of the Cadillac and put Darla into the back seat of his cruiser, which was separated from the front by a wire mesh screen. Knowing that common criminals often sat there, she thought this was a little too severe.

"I didn't steal the car," she said, leaning forward to make sure he heard her.

The patrol car was already running. He dropped it into gear and started to drive. "We'll get your statement as soon as you've had your rights read to you at the station. Just sit back and enjoy the ride."

She sat back, scowling, not enjoying anything, then leaned forward, again. "I want you to know one thing right off the bat before I get involved in this over my head," she said. "I only found the body. I had nothing to do with stabbing him, and I don't know who he is. I was jogging, and I heard him scream. End of *that* story."

He hit the brakes hard and whipped his head around so fast that his blue hat almost spun in a circle. "What body?"

"The one back there in the woods." She motioned with her head. "All I did was find the guy. I answered the reward ad in the paper, and the guy who picked me up was driving that red Cadillac. I am an innocent bystander."

He made a dour face at her. "If you're making this up, it isn't funny."

"I can show you," she said.

He spun the wheel and slewed around in a tight U-turn, the tires squealing loudly on the wet road. Darla bounced around in the back, trying to stay erect with her hands cuffed behind her back. This was not the first time she had worn handcuffs, but it was also not something one could get used to easily. She watched as the officer got back on the radio to report this latest twist. She hoped the cops would get so busy with the murder that they would overlook her driving-a-stolen-car infraction in the confusion—at least long enough to give her time to run. As yet they did not even know her name, which was going to remain Darla Dalton for as long as that alias was useful.

"Guide me there," he barked at her.

"Drive past two roads on the left," she shouted above the noise of the engine. "Then turn into a country lane a mile or two from here."

He nodded. Now *he* was speeding. Who was the criminal here?

She rolled her eyes. Presently he found the lane and took it at a more sensible pace. "Just there on the right," she told him.

He stopped and got out. "I don't see anything."

She ducked down, trying to find his face as he stood there in the rain. "There's like a little hill and some briers. The body's on the other side."

Now he leaned down to look at her. "This better not be a joke."

She swore it with her eyes.

"Okay." He opened her door and helped her out. With a hand firmly in the crook of her elbow he escorted her while they both got wet. The leaves were slick, and she almost went down once, but he was a strong and agile young man. She wondered, quite stupidly, if he might have fifty thousand bucks lying around somewhere at home.

"You can see his shirt from here," she said. "Over there."

"Stay put," he told her.

She watched him pick his way forward, dodging brambles and burrs. At the crest of the little rise he stopped, then took another few steps. Then he dropped out of sight as if a trapdoor had opened under his feet—squatting down beside the body, apparently. For very few reasons she felt good about the way this was turning out. She had finally done her civic duty, and the cop knew she wasn't a liar. That would be good when all the other cops and the forensic experts got here. She could talk her way out of the cuffs long enough to spend a moment alone behind a tree—even this efficient young man had to respect her privacy—and sneak away. She hoped.

The cop hurried back, grim-faced. She could read the name tag on his jacket as he neared: Officer Rogers.

"Stay put," he snapped again as he charged past her, making a beeline for his car. He sat inside and talked on the radio. She thought very hard about running away, but no, that would be insane. With cuffs on, she would be prey to every hazard this woods had to offer, beast or man. She doubted that she would get lost, but the feeling of helplessness caused by the cuffs was overwhelming. Plus they were hurting her wrists already.

She waited without much patience for what seemed like an inordinate amount of time. When he finally got done, her black hair was dripping wet and her dress was glued to her skin; with all the rain on her glasses her world had become a fishbowl full of bubbles. And they said a little rain never hurt anybody.

He marched up to her, his face creased by the weight of his thoughts. "Describe the man who picked you up in the Cadillac," he said.

"You won't believe me," she replied immediately. "He looked just like the chief of police, Jackson Goodrow. He said he was his brother."

"Uh-huh. Do you know what that substance is that's smeared all over the radio? And the yellow powder?"

She shrugged. "Not a clue. I didn't touch it, though."

"It was there when he picked you up?"

"Yes."

"Where is he now?"

Once again she had to use her head to indicate a direction. "He went over there to check out the body. Then he told me to wait in the car while he went up the slope. That was at least forty-five minutes ago. I got scared alone so I drove off."

He frowned to himself. "Was he armed?"

"Not that I saw. He was actually very nice."

He thought for a moment, his frown deepening. "Hold on one more second," he said and went back to his car. Again he ducked inside, but this time he returned fairly soon. "Okay," he said, and got behind her. He unlocked the cuffs; they dropped away. "The owner of the Cadillac is at HQ blowing off steam. From what they can understand, a lone thief carjacked it downtown, tossed him right out of it. That goopy stuff was dripping off his face, and it's been found in other places. We don't know what it is, but we do know that the chief of police does not have a brother, so your man was an impostor. One of our detectives is after this guy already, and he's on the way. I want you to get inside my vehicle, lock it securely, and lie down on the front seat. If you hear gunshots, you're to lie on the floor. When the backup unit arrives, you'll have to lead them to the body."

He turned and jogged into the woods, leaving her in confusion. She knew for sure that one more prediction for today would have been in her horoscope, had she bothered to read it this morning: "You will become a key witness in a murder case."

She did not know whether to laugh, cry, or steal the patrol car and head for the border.

CHAPTER

26

Haven't I Seen You Before?

I heard a scream," Darkman said to the fat man. Blood was pounding hotly in his ears, thumping in his neck like an extra heartbeat. The need to kill this fellow was almost overwhelming, but it would have to wait. There were plenty more cult members downstairs. By envisioning them as a heap of corpses he was able to rein in his fury at what they had done. He would get them, every one of them. He had to squeeze his eyes shut with the effort of will it took to remain calm, to think his way through this instead of attacking blindly. They all had guns; against shotgun shells even his rage could not win.

"Give her to me," the fat man said with a marked lack of patience. The noise of people and music downstairs forced him to raise his voice. He leaned his shotgun against the wall. "Go back down and party with the others like you're supposed to. You'll have your chance with her later."

Shaking inside, barely able to control his breathing, Darkman rolled Shawna into his waiting arms. *Give it time,* his inner voice recommended, the best advice it had come up with in a long time. He jammed his fists into his pockets and stalked away.

"Hold up," the fat man suddenly commanded.

Darkman swung around.

"You don't look familiar. How long have you been with the flock?"

Darkman shrugged, grinned. "Not very long. Joe just sponsored me."

"Ah." His frown relaxed. "What happened to your equipment?"

"I, uh . . . oh, I forgot. It's in there." He ducked past him and collected his bottle and gun from the bedroom, then returned, smiling like a simpleton while relief washed through his mind. This guy obviously did not know the face of the chief of police. Maybe he was new in town. But would anyone downstairs recognize Goodrow? With the sermon over, they might start looking at faces, start getting concerned.

Give it time.

He walked past the fat man and went to the stairway. To his relief more of the lights downstairs had been turned off, making the scene look even more like a disco, colored lights flashing here and there, the strobe flickering away. What this insane drinking and dancing had to do with young girls and tattooed young men he could not guess.

He went down the stairs and wormed his way across the huge room, being battered and slammed and whacked by rifles and bottles on the way. The heat inside was rising from the sweating, overheated dancers. At the far wall he sidled into the darkest shadow he could find. Where Brother Hopewell had gone, he did not know, but he doubted that the preacher was off praying somewhere. The aura of opulence made Darkman assume that Hopewell was just another shyster out for some easy bucks.

How had this phony evangelist brainwashed these people? Darkman wondered. Did his success have something to do with their being old? Weren't the lion's share of TV evangelists' followers and donors older people?

Hopewell's followers were old men, by and large. Old and rich. Were they trying to dance their way to a long life? And did their advanced age make them less guilty? He thought not. They were old enough to know better.

He raised his shotgun and examined it. It had a kind of spring-loaded door on the side where you were supposed to shove some shells in. Wouldn't it be nice if he had some? About forty of them? What would happen if he just opened fire in here?

One big mess.

He found himself utterly at a loss as to what he should do next. His primary mission was to rescue Shawna, but from the looks of this celebration, she was in little danger at the moment. If they performed their ceremonies here in the mansion—if there even was a ceremony today— when would it begin? Questions, questions. He was tired of unanswered questions.

A feeble old man was doing a solo Bristol stomp in front of him. Darkman put his things down and got a handful of the back of his jacket and hauled him close, hoping he was too old to remember the chief's face. "What time does the ceremony start?" he bawled into his hearing aid.

He received a toothless grin. "Same time as usual, I guess."

"And what time is that?"

Now he frowned with suspicion. "Haven't you ever been here before?"

Darkman tapped his head. "I can't remember much."

"I used to have that problem," the man bellowed, tapping his own head. "Now my mind is as clear as a bell."

And dumber than hell, Darkman thought nastily. "So what time?"

"It's always been midnight, but since this is a special meeting, who knows? Hey, look at this!"

Darkman watched as the old man put his rifle and bottle down and starting beating his chest like Tarzan. The urge to kill him was strong, but he just nodded and smiled until Tarzan had a coughing fit and staggered away.

Midnight, then. No way would his face last that long. He should have simply killed the fat guy and hurried away with Shawna. Perhaps it was not too late.

He gathered up his belongings and worked his way through the mob to the stairway. He climbed it, not very concerned about being seen, and strode down the hallway. He had little choice as to what to do now: he would kill the fat man, pick Shawna up, march through the crowd with her as if he knew what he was doing, escape into the woods, and try to find Darla Dalton and the Cadillac. The plan made sense.

He came to the bedroom door and stopped. Somebody was still moving around inside. He could hear Shawna whimpering now. For the last time he discarded the bottle and shotgun. He put his hand on the knob, took a breath, let it out, rethought the plan. It would be him against a loaded shotgun. But why would the man still be carrying his weapon around? He was safe in there, obviously a leader of sorts in this crazy outfit, and had likely put the gun down someplace.

Darkman turned the knob. The door was locked. He put more effort into it, using a fraction of his anger, twisted it until it crunched, then slammed the door open with a shoulder.

The fat guy looked up, alarm transforming his face into the wrinkled visage of a pig. He was sitting on the bed with a pile of votive candles and a small perforated box between his legs; his shotgun lay on the floor beside one of the dressers. Shawna had been tied to the bedposts again. In one hand he held a slender jar half full of bugs. As Darkman took this all in, one of the bugs jumped out of the bottle and hopped across the bed.

A shiny brown cricket.

"You son of a bitch," Darkman breathed. His police-chief hands formed claws. If the color of his face could have changed, it would have been as white as the pillow the cricket was bounding across in its panic. In an instant Darkman was hoisting the man up by the neck and hurling him across the room. He smashed against a dresser, and it burst into jagged shards of lumber. Crickets escaped from the rolling jar and scurried for the baseboards in terror. Darkman jumped at the man again, hauled him up. The fat man screamed. A thin spear of wood had pierced his left earlobe like a grotesque African earring. Blood drizzled down his neck. Darkman saw it all through a numbing haze of red.

He threw him again. This time the man slammed into a wall and rebounded while framed pictures slid down the other walls and crashed to the floor. The wall would bear the scars of that blow for a long time: a man-shaped depression was smashed into the plaster. Darkman hoisted the fat man again, needing to see blood. He raked his fingers across the man's face. The artificial skin on his fingers peeled sloppily open, baring the sharp twigs of his bones. Four deep gashes were carved into his flabby cheek; the man screamed while his blood squirted out in bright red streams. Two of the gashes had cut all the way through his cheek into his mouth. He spit out a thick glob of blood, his face twisted and gray, his eyes squeezed shut. The tip of his tongue was poking through one of the slits.

"Now," Darkman heard himself shriek as he lifted him again, *"you die!"*

But he didn't die. Hopewell in his ghastly red robe had appeared at the door and had raised a shotgun, aimed directly at Shawna. "Put him down!" he shouted.

Darkman froze, his head snapping back and forth, his rage a grotesque monster writhing inside his stomach and his brain.

"Now!"

He dropped the fat man, who rolled over once on the floor and sat up, squalling like a baby. But Darkman needed to see more than just pain. He needed to see someone die—anyone but Shawna, Julie's niece. His mouth was as dry as ashes, his heart whumping out a manic beat.

"You're the—you're the chief of police!" Hopewell blurted, almost choking on the words, his eyebrows jerking up with monumental surprise. "How in the hell did you find us?"

Darkman hurriedly hid his splitting hands behind his back. Being Goodrow had worked to his advantage this time. Hopewell would not casually gun down a cop; he would never gun down the chief of police. Unless he was crazy.

"The place is surrounded," Darkman croaked through his parched throat. "The insanity is over."

The fat man was staggering dazedly to his feet, both hands clamped to his mangled face. "Chief of police?" he gurgled, and spit out more blood. "We've got to run, Norm. Rio—"

"Look out the window," Hopewell shouted. "See if there are any cops out there!"

"Rio—"

"Forget Rio, Fritz! Look outside!"

He wobbled to the drapes and shoved them apart. As his head swiveled back and forth, he jerked the large splinter out of his earlobe, then turned. "I don't see any cops. Maybe they're hiding."

"Check the hallway. Look out front."

Fritz went out on his shaking legs, leaving a trail of blood on the carpet. He was back in ten seconds. "Nothing but fancy cars, and they all look familiar."

Hopewell's eyes jerked over to Darkman. "Frisk him."

Fritz bumbled over and patted bloody handprints all over Darkman's clothes. "Nothing."

"Good." Hopewell looked at Fritz, then back. "Get your gun and shoot him."

Fritz's eyes became suddenly clearer. He stood up straighter. "Shoot the chief of police? Not me."

"Do it."

"Uh-uh." Fritz backed away from Hopewell. "Cop-killing means a guaranteed conviction, a certain death penalty. You shoot him."

"Do it!"

"No!"

Hopewell ground his teeth, his eyes flashing. "Son of a bitch!" he snarled at Darkman. "What am I going to do with you? Of all the screwed-up, stupid things! Jesus!"

Darkman stared at him while his heart went on thumping. At this moment he felt impervious to shotguns, rifles, bullets, bombs, nukes, anything.

"Wait," Fritz panted. "Make the faithful kill him. Make his death a part of the ceremony."

Hopewell twitched his head slightly. "They'll run like jackals when they realize who he is. Even *they* aren't *that* stupid."

"We can put a bag over his head, then stab him like we did Flynn."

Hopewell put on an expression of self-pity. "Christ, why does everything have to be so damn complicated?" He fumed silently for a moment. "You set it up, Fritz. Him first, then the girl. We'll get both of them out of the way forever."

Fritz looked at his blood-slick hands. "I'm in no shape to carry her downstairs. I'm bleeding like a stuck pig."

"Then make Goodrow drag her around. I'll divert the flock's attention. And when this day's over, we'll *both* go to Rio, at least until all of this blows over."

He handed the shotgun over to Fritz. "Give me a minute to move the flock to one of the other rooms. Set these two up in the cottage so we can finish this fast."

Fritz took the gun. "We could just pack up and head for Rio now, and screw the rest of it."

Hopewell turned on him. "He's seen us, probably heard our names! Use your head!" He stomped out.

Fritz opened a dresser drawer, never letting his eyes leave Darkman, hauled out a handful of garments, and tossed a T-shirt at Darkman, who made no move to catch it. "Pull it over your head," he commanded him. Blood continued to rain onto Fritz's belly, some of it dripping down onto his shoes. He edged over to Shawna and jerked at her restraints, holding the barrel against her neck.

Her eyes fluttered shut just as Darkman noticed they were open. Had she been faking unconsciousness? Could he count on her to create a diversion if an opportunity showed itself?

When she was untied, Fritz straightened and motioned at Darkman. "Pull the shirt over your head, dammit."

Darkman picked it up, hiding his shredded fingers in its folds. He worked it clumsily over his head. It was possible to see through it well enough to get around.

"Pick her up. If you do anything stupid, I'll blow a big hole right through her head."

Darkman stuck out his arms and pretended to stumble blindly toward the bed, his hands balled into fists. He got his arms under her and hoisted her up. If she was awake, she didn't let on. He could see Fritz looking at his watch, could hear him muttering to himself.

One of Shawna's arms was dangling near his knees, and she gave him a pinch, once, twice, three times.

So she really was awake. And he could see. Fritz still thought he was the chief of police. Add that up, he thought, and what do you get?

One slim chance.

"Let's go," Fritz said.

They went.

CHAPTER

27

In the Limelight

With the rain came a gusting wind that threatened to snap off the tops of trees. Even through the T-shirt Darkman's eyes were battered by huge windblown drops of rain while the billowing fabric flapped against his artificial ears as loud as wet sheets pitching and tossing on a clothesline. He noticed that Shawna's eyelids were jerking reflexively under the rainfall. He clutched her tighter to his chest so that Fritz could not see her face and she would be more comfortable.

Hunched against the shifting rain, they skirted the mansion and tromped past the body of the elderly gent propped up against the wall with blood washing down his chin. Darkman saw Fritz look over at him and then turn away, apparently unconcerned. In his baggy suit with his thin hair tousled and his tie blowing like a rope in the wind, Fritz resembled a sour-faced door-to-door shotgun salesman hiking home after a particularly bad day. Darkman was weaving from side to side as if blind, his feet sloshing through the soggy grass, trying to seem utterly puzzled, hoping for obstacles to blunder against, of which none appeared. He was aware with his limited vision that something was looming ahead, some white thing that he eventually recognized as a house with a reddish tiled roof. Dead thornbushes around it indicated a flower bed left to fend for itself too long. He plotted a path straight into it.

"Cut to the right a little," Fritz said.

Darkman eased left.

"The right, dammit. The other way. There's a cottage up ahead."

"I'm spending the night?" Darkman asked in a voice shot through with sarcasm.

"There's a sidewalk coming up."

He stumbled onto it and attempted to walk into the wall.

Fritz took ahold of his sleeve and jerked him roughly. "The things I gotta do," he muttered. He edged ahead and swung the door open. "You can thank your lucky stars you're not a blind man for a living," he grunted. "Keep walking."

Darkman went inside. In the gloom he could smell the waxy traces of old candle smoke. Fritz flipped a switch and a lone spotlight snapped on at the other end of the room, throwing a sharp circle of light on a shiny metal table with canvas straps hanging from it. Darkman felt his flesh crawl. Terrified little girls had been dragged into this barnlike house, had been burned with candles and defiled by countless men.

"Keep going," Fritz said, and poked him in the back with his shotgun. Darkman stumbled forward with his head high, imitating the way people tended to walk when they could not see. Fortunately the T-shirt permitted better viewing than a blindfold would have. He neared the table and walked into its cold steel edge with a lurch.

"Walk around that thing and put the girl down on the floor behind it," Fritz ordered.

"What is it?"

"Your bed for the next few minutes," Fritz answered tiredly. "Go on, do it."

Darkman groped his way around the table, still using

his fists so that his tattered fingers couldn't be seen, and gently lowered Shawna down behind it. He gave her arm an encouraging squeeze before he straightened.

"It's a table," Fritz said. "Lie down on it."

"What if I say no?"

"Then she dies, you die, and I'm done with this charade forever."

"I thought you didn't want to kill a cop."

"Not in front of witnesses."

"But you'd kill a little girl anytime."

Fritz jabbed the shotgun hard into his chest. "I've heard enough sermons to last me a lifetime, Chief. I only do what has to be done. Lie down."

"I'm not tired."

Darkman saw him jerk, saw a swinging shadow trace a line toward his own face. The barrel cracked loudly across his cheek and knocked him sideways a bit. Rage flared, hot as acid in his thoughts.

"Do it."

Darkman sat on the table.

"Stretch out."

He did it, savoring the rage, controlling it like a bubble of finely blown glass. Fritz set the gun aside and began strapping him down, grunting as he yanked the buckles tight. Darkman welcomed the restraints, the tighter the better. "That kid lived for a while," he said.

"What kid?"

"The skinny guy. The one with the tattoos. He crawled halfway down the mountain."

Fritz paused. "That's how you found us."

"Bingo. And I'm not the only one."

Fritz was silent.

"You can cut a deal with the D.A., immunity for testimony. Let me and the girl go. We can be in the D.A.'s house in an hour. The cult fries, you walk."

Fritz snorted and went back to the straps. "I can't believe a police chief can be so naive and such a liar at the same time. That tells me you've watched too many cop shows since they parked you behind a desk. I've got priors half a mile long, outstanding warrants in four states. I walk out of this one, I wind up extradited to the next."

"Might beat waiting around for my men to show up and gun you down."

"Either you think I'm stupid, or it's you who is," Fritz said. He checked the straps, nodded, and stepped away. "Why would you walk up here and leave the rookies behind? Since when does a police chief do all the footwork?"

"New policy."

"Right. You were probably walking your goddamn dog when you tripped over Flynn's worthless carcass. Do us both a kindness and shut the hell up."

"It's your funeral," Darkman muttered.

The inner voice had a word to add: *Don't scare him all the way to death, Darkman!*

"Aw, shut up," Darkman muttered.

"You shut up," Fritz snapped. He moved behind the table to look down at Shawna, then glanced at his watch. "Well, it's been real fun, but I've got to catch a midnight flight on the Rio express. Chief, you have a nice life."

"What, no candles between my toes?" Darkman said, knowing quite well that the candles and the bugs were still up in the bedroom, victims of the change in plans. "Whose idiotic idea was this whole farce, Fritz? Who dreamed it up? You or the other nut?"

Fritz ignored him. He picked up the shotgun and walked away. It was hard to follow his dark, bobbing shape with the spotlight shining in his eyes, but Darkman could hear his footfalls move out into the rain and fade away.

"Shawna?" he said into the echoing silence that was backgrounded only by rain beating on the roof. He turned his head to the side, frowning inside the T-shirt. "Shawna?"

No response. This time she had passed out for real.

Maybe that was for the best, he reasoned. What happened next was going to be messy, no matter which way it turned out.

He began to strain against the straps, guiding and molding the rage that might save him, picturing the things he needed to see, remembering the things he needed to remember, the fuel for his hate.

And soon, in the distance and coming fast in the gathering dark, a sound.

Chanting.

The pretty woman who had never really been Darla Dalton heard no sirens before the cops arrived like a regiment of blue and white cavalry. They braked to a stop in the mud around the cruiser in which she was unhappily waiting, and an army of blue-shirts jumped out, some of them carrying rifles. Had they sent this whole search party just for Gilligan? she wondered as she stepped out into the rain. Fortunately it was beginning to slack off, though the clouds were still low and black. She pushed the door shut as a cop with yellow stripes on his sleeves marched up.

"You the one?" he demanded.

A witty reply struck her; she held it in. "Yes."

"Where's the body?"

"Up that way." She pointed. "Over that hump by the brambles."

He motioned to his men. They all scurried off behind him.

"Nice to meet you too," she mumbled, crossing her arms. It was getting chilly, though the wind was easing a little. She looked around uncertainly. Since everyone was traipsing off into the woods, she no longer had any reason to be here, unless she wanted to wait around to get officially arrested for driving a stolen car or for fraternizing with a possible murderer. For a crazy moment as the police charged up the slope, following a trail she doubted was there anymore, she thought about checking the dead man to see if maybe he had money in his pockets, or maybe an expensive watch she might not have noticed. How about a checkbook?

How else could she get her hands on fifty thousand dollars in a hurry? If it was just her own freedom on the line she could run away from it all, but it wasn't just her and she had nowhere to go.

She had waited beside the car for a little less than fifteen long, undecisive minutes when another car roared up, this one a drab green, with three people inside. One passenger was a woman with blondish hair and a slightly green look, as if she had just swallowed a bug. They all got out, and the older-looking fellow, the one with the word "cop" written all over his face, hurried over to Darla.

"What's happening?" he said.

She shrugged. "All the other policemen took off up the slope," she said. "I guess they're trying to follow the trail."

He nodded. "Where is the body?"

Once again she gave directions. He trotted away. Darla gave the other woman an apprehensive little wave, and she wandered over. The man with her was tall and somber. She noticed that the word stamped upon his face was "money."

"I'm just hanging around," she said. "Glad the rain quit."

"Yes," the man said.

The woman was looking at the plainsclothes cop. She shifted her attention. "My name's Julie Hastings," she said, "and this is Martin Clayborne. Was there a man here?"

"Lots of men," Darla replied, stashing the name Clayborne into a mental Rolodex for later consultation.

"A civilian, I mean."

"Just a guy named Gilligan. He said he was the police chief's brother, and he sure looked like it, but it turns out the police chief doesn't have a brother."

Julie glanced at Martin, who replied with a shrug. "Where did he go?" she asked.

"The same place everybody else went." Darla pointed. "Up that way."

The cop was coming back. "I know this area," he said. "There's only one house up there. It's just like the others built here—very expensive."

"That doesn't disqualify the owners from suspicion," Martin Clayborne said. "But what would Peyton Westlake have to do with any of this?"

"Maybe nothing, maybe a lot," the cop said. "The red Cadillac has what is very likely his artificial skin all over the inside. Some of it has already turned to dust." He looked at Darla. "That's what I was told."

"Well, the stuff isn't really *all over* the car," she said. "It could be Silly Putty or something."

He jerked one eyebrow up a notch. "Are you covering for him?"

"Me?" She pressed a hand to her throat. "I barely know Gilligan."

Now both eyebrows went up. "Gilligan? Like the island?"

"Yeah, the skipper, the professor, Mary Ann . . . you know."

"Very unimaginative." The cop shifted his gaze to Julie. "Was Westlake fond of 'Gilligan's Island' reruns?"

Martin Clayborne rolled his eyes. "This is stupid. Why did you drag us out here? Peyton Westlake is dead."

Darla frowned. "Who's he?"

The cop waved a hand, signaling everybody to shut up. "Christ, just get into my car. I want to talk to the people up the hill, see if they've found anything. And, Julie, what will happen if I try to pull Westlake's face off?"

Darla stopped halfway into a step toward the car. "His *what?*"

"His face."

"I have no idea what you're talking about," Julie said.

Darla agreed. "That makes two of us."

"Oh, put a lid on it," the cop growled, and they went wordlessly to the car and got in for the short ride up the mountain.

CHAPTER

28

Aladdin's Lamp

They filed inside, these men and women whose minds had been rearranged by the power of Hopewell's eloquence. They were garbed in eerie sackcloth robes, and they carried candles that had been extinguished by the wind and the rain. Their shotguns were clutched uneasily in their hands or propped on their shoulders. Their faces were shadowed voids beneath their hoods, and they were murmuring the nonsense they had been taught while rainwater dripped from their robes and made puddles on the floor.

Darkman was thinking about Popeye sucking spinach through his pipe when all seemed lost. How did he do that?

Hopewell came in under the protection of two umbrellas held over his head by a couple of worshipers. One of them pulled the door shut. The crowd parted as their Moses glided through. He stopped and looked down at Darkman, then leaned over to check on Shawna.

In his eyes Darkman saw only nervousness and petty fears. Some guru.

He turned and raised his arms. Darkman saw something silvery flash as he did—the old shotgun-in-one-hand, knife-up-the-other-sleeve trick. "My beloved children," he intoned solemnly over the sound of the worshipers' wheezing lungs and loud coughs, a result of their exposure to the damp weather. "This is the ceremony of ceremonies, the Ceremony of Youthful Unity."

He stepped aside with a sweep of his arms and let everyone have a good look at the first course on tonight's menu of madness: a man in a soggy business suit and a wet red tie, with a T-shirt over his head, strapped down on an operating table. Darkman scowled.

"Hear the words of God," he thundered. "Here lies a traitor from among us, one who would defy the gods, who would ruin us all and steal our immortality!"

The crowd grew restive, looking around, trying to figure out who had betrayed them. Darkman had to admit this was a clever ploy by Hopewell. After watching *him* get butchered no one would dare rebel.

At this point Hopewell launched into another version of the sermon he had given inside the mansion. Darkman had already broken the straps on the side where Shawna lay hidden behind the metal skirt of the table, but he could scarcely afford to finish the job with half a hundred people watching. How long this newest harangue might last he could not know, but he was willing to wait for a moment when the flock, overcome by the power of their faith, would start to gyrate and foam and whirl like the crowd in any revival tent, if the preacher is good, and Hopewell sure was. Too bad he hadn't become a politician; he'd have been thrown in jail a long time ago.

It was then that two things happened that would mark, in Darkman's memory, this night for a long time to come, as if it were not already memorable enough. First, he heard Shawna moan as she regained consciousness. Second, he smelled something burning.

His face.

Later he would ponder how strange and wondrous this must have looked to the superstitious faithful, the sight of a man in business attire whose hooded face was suddenly wreathed in yellow smoke, whose fisted hands suddenly burst into roiling yellow clouds. It was then, just as Darkman's dormant energy ignited and he snapped the remaining straps like masking tape, that there rose from the crowd a cry of awe.

Hopewell stopped shouting when he realized that something behind him had diverted their attention from his speech; he spun around so hard his hood fell back to reveal his face and disheveled hair. His eyes widened to the size of salad bowls.

Darkman swung into a sitting position and ripped the T-shirt away, a malevolent genie fresh out of a Persian bottle, his face boiling with smoke so sulfurous that it could have been vented from a volcano that opened into hell. He spread his bubbling lips and emitted a dark and evil laugh that sent the weakest of the faithful stampeding for the door.

He jumped to his feet. "Now *see* the devil!" he shrieked, enjoying this. He raised his hands; twin jets of yellow exhaust followed them in an upward arc. "Bow down to me!" he bellowed while his face dripped in strings. "Bow down to the powers of hell!"

Many of the worshipers were uninclined to stick around for this. Shotguns clattered to the floor. People got bowled over in the stampede and screamed as they were trampled. With one hand Darkman swiped more dying skin from his face, exposing bone and gumless teeth. *"Die!"* he roared, making menacing gestures. The single doorway was stopped up like a bottle. People scrambled up the writhing mountain of bodies like ants up an anthill, insane with terror, screaming, clawing as they slid back down and tried again.

Hopewell turned around. "Fritz!" he shouted. *"Fritz! Where are you?"* He spun around again, this time in a complete circle. "My children! Wait!" He began to flap his arms wildly. The knife flew out of his sleeve and shot through the room. It impaled someone squarely in the back. The victim clawed at it as he fell over. Now Darkman saw blood.

Red blood.

He grinned. His head had begun to thud as his rage took over, a dark horse galloping through his mind, leaving hoofprints filled with acid. He was dimly aware that Hopewell had fired his shotgun overhead in an effort to stop the exodus. A shower of plaster rained to the floor, belching a cloud of white dust into the air. Darkman saw the preacher jerk around and pump another shell into the chamber. *Boom!* One of his faithful caught the brunt of the buckshot with the side of his face. Blood and bits of flesh sprayed over the people and the walls.

Hopewell, bellowing something unintelligible, began to fire indiscriminately into the crowd. He had become a psychotic killer. Following another boom, the spotlight was knocked askew to illuminate the doorway, where several dead people stared at nothing. Candles, eyeglasses, and discarded robes were strewn on the bloody carpet.

One of the faithful, perhaps a veteran of some long-ago war, dropped to his knees and leveled his shotgun at Darkman. His eyes were wide and terrified, but he seemed to know what he was doing. Darkman jumped behind the operating table just as Shawna was sitting up. He pushed her head back down, but not before she had seen his face.

The gun roared. Buckshot clanged against the sheet metal of the table's skirt.

Tangled in her sheet, she screamed and tried to scramble away.

Darkman grabbed her in a bear hug and pressed his face to her ear. "I'm a friend of your aunt Julie," he barked above the chaos and the noise. "Keep down and don't look at me. Aunt Julie will explain all of this to you later."

Shawna nodded, knocking the back of her head against his exposed skull. A fair amount of smoke still followed his movements. He looked up and saw the kneeling veteran banging on his gun with one open hand. It had jammed on him.

"Another K mart special," Darkman muttered. He tensed himself and launched into a somersault across the floor, shot to his feet again, and scrambled for a nearby shotgun, hoping it was loaded.

The veteran had his weapon working again, but Darkman pumped his shotgun and fired first. The veteran was knocked sideways by the blow.

Darkman turned his attention back to the preacher just as Hopewell threw his shotgun at him. It boomeranged across the room, and Darkman ducked. Somebody behind him yelped.

Now Hopewell leaped behind the table. He rose up a second later with one arm hooked around Shawna's neck. In his fright and confusion he exposed his real self as a crazy, terrified little man working hard on a double chin. It struck Darkman that except for Hopewell's glittering, flashing eyes, he could have been the brother of Peyton Westlake's tax-time CPA. How could anyone follow this fellow and believe his teachings?

"I'll break her neck, whatever you are!" he screeched at Darkman. "I can do it!"

Darkman saw Shawna's eyes flutter open for a moment. She looked at him, but there was no fear of him in her expression. In this mayhem, he realized, she had only him to trust now, no matter how awful he looked. He swung his shotgun up and pointed it at Hopewell's face, every ounce of his rage demanding to see him dead. No good. Half the load would strike Shawna. He reined his feelings tighter.

Suddenly he felt two cold, unyielding metal cylinders being pressed against the back of his neck. He didn't need the evening paper to figure things out. Not everyone in a bad situation panics all the way. Some of Hopewell's faithful still had their wits.

Hopewell looked crazier and more vicious than ever now as he gaped at the well-dressed incarnation of Satan that was Darkman unmasked. It struck Darkman that perhaps now, for the first time, Hopewell actually believed all of his own absurd teachings about gods and devils.

"Kill it!" he shouted over the noise, then jerked his free arm to indicate the wall of people still fighting to escape. His eyes were shiny and insane. "Kill it, and then kill them all! Do you hear me? *Kill it and then kill them all!*"

CHAPTER

29

Exit Stage Left

I see it like this," Detective Weatherspoon said as he drove.

Julie and Martin were in the back; Darla Dalton had the pleasure of riding in the front seat beside the tall, thin, and somewhat unpleasant detective in the cheap suit who had the power to arrest her if he only knew her troubles. She was monumentally unhappy. Weatherspoon's big Chrysler had an engine, but that was about it, as far as luxury went. It seemed to Darla that if she were to push him out and steal this tub, she might get a couple hundred bucks for it on the market. Why did cops, from Columbo to Hunter to Charlie's Angels, always drive such broken-down wheels?

"How do you see it?" Julie said coldly from the back seat.

"Westlake got his revenge on the thugs who shot his assistant and blew up his laboratory by the river. He got the taste of blood and couldn't let it go. I've seen that happen before. With his skin invention he can look like anybody he wants, except maybe a woman. Hah!"

Dead silence. Weatherspoon looked slyly at Darla,

raking his gaze up and down her tight, wet clothes. "If you're Peyton Westlake, I'm Donald Duck," he said, and performed a solo laugh.

She saw no hint of easy money in his face and worked on ignoring him. She knew quite well that she was becoming very mercenary, seeing people only in terms of how much money she could get out of them, but this was her own private war against some very powerful people, and in wartime you do what you have to, especially if a life is on the line and that life belongs to someone close to you. She shifted around and looked at Martin, whose eight-hundred-dollar suit fairly shouted out tales of credit cards and cash. "So," she said, "what might you have to do with this?"

"I'm a hostage," he replied sourly.

She hesitated, wanting to prolong the conversation tactfully and without sounding like a gold digger. "Are you two an item?" she asked, hating the sound of it.

Julie gave her a distracted glance. "Huh?"

"You two." She made sketches with her hands. "Are you married?"

Julie shook her head, and Darla suppressed an urge to throw herself into Martin's lap. He was a good-looking guy, and Darla figured she had Julie beat in the looks department. Julie was kind of ragged around the edges, as if she hadn't been sleeping much lately. "So," Darla said to him, "which one of the local skyscrapers do you own?"

"Hmm?"

"Here it is," Weatherspoon said, taking a left turn onto a street that had no name. He immediately jammed on the brakes.

He should have had his headlights on, Darla thought, looking to see what he had almost run over.

It was a monk. A lady monk. She was crawling along the wet street on her hands and knees. Blood was running down her face in two thin lines. One of her sneakers was dragging along behind her foot by the laces.

Weatherspoon sat up straighter. "What in the hell?"

The car was suddenly surrounded by a horde of monks. He snapped the headlights on, and everyone in the car gawked as the stampede trundled past. Some of the monks would fall down, get up, run some more, trip on their robes, and fall again. A lot of cars were trying to exit a long, narrow driveway, but they became tangled and blocked as they smashed into one another. Monks were abandoning them in a honking, shouting frenzy. Broken glass littered the ground.

Weatherspoon jerked a fat red emergency light from under the dash, then rolled down his window, stuck the light on the roof, and it began to sweep the area with bright red beams. Then he turned the siren on. The monks seemed alarmed by this. They scattered and charged into the blustery dark, skidding on the grass and blundering into the hedges.

Darla turned to Weatherspoon. "Costume party?"

"No." He sounded both grim and satisfied as he shouted above the scream of the siren. "I suspected something like this." He pushed his door open and stuck a hand inside his jacket. A large pistol made an appearance. "It's a satanic cult," he hollered, looking toward the mansion that bulked up at the end of the winding drive. "But I would never have expected to find it in this affluent neighborhood."

He ducked back inside momentarily and looked at Julie, a smug expression on his face. "Looks like your dead boyfriend is in the cult business," he said. "He's probably the head honcho."

She made small negative motions with her head.

Darla tried to put two and two together. Gillian was a monk with a Silly Putty face you could pull off and smear on a car stereo? And he was pretending to be the police chief's brother after stealing a car and taking off a dead man's shoes to look at his toes while being the head honcho of a satanic monastery? This time two and two equaled about eleven and a half point nine to the twelfth power.

Everyone was getting out of the Chrysler. Weatherspoon began shouting at the monks, with no effect. Darla watched while he and Julie and Martin tore off across the lawn toward the big house, Julie bobbling along in her high heels while Martin tried to help her keep her balance.

Most of the monks had passed by now. Darla decided to get out. She opened her door, but immediately changed her mind and shut it.

The only thing she knew for certain in this confusion was that she needed fifty thousand dollars in the next twenty-four hours or her brother would be pushing up ferns in a jungle half a world away, killed by his own people for the crime of having trusted someone a little too much. It was an old story, one that had played out in her head a thousand times, and the final scene was always this: she had to get some money—lots of money, fifty grand—or he would die. The end.

She slid across the seat and took hold of the steering wheel. The police radio started blotting and squawking some noisy gibberish, and she fiddled with the knobs to make it shut up. When it was quiet she ripped the red light off the roof and threw it on the floor. "One way or another," she muttered through her gritted teeth while the revolving light splashed her face with a red glow. "I'm getting out of this mess."

She slammed the gearshift into drive and pressed the accelerator to the floor, wildly cranking the steering wheel while the rear tires spit out hissing geysers of mud.

CHAPTER

30

Your Place or Mine?

With two cold shotgun barrels pressed to the back of his neck, Darkman rose up. Pretty much out of options, he let his own recently borrowed gun thump to the floor. One of the faithful behind him had only to pull the trigger, and he would become the Headless Darkman, searching for his private Sleepy Hollow for the rest of eternity.

"Kill it!" Hopewell shrieked again. A line of drool was sliding down his chin as he puffed and panted from all the exertion of the last few minutes. "Kill everybody!"

Darkman sensed the pressure against his neck easing. Even Hopewell's own followers were seeing him as the twisted toad he really was. Like Jim Jones, he wanted to go out in a blaze of bloodshed.

Darkman turned around. The two men backed away a step, their eyes huge and afraid of what they were seeing, the skeletal face of death and their own hallowed leader noisily going mad. "Put the guns down," he said gently. The bottleneck of people at the door was breaking apart, most of the flock escaping into the dark, leaving twelve or

213

thirteen behind, some of them silent in death, some of them whimpering, still trying to crawl away.

One woman's eyes flicked up at something new behind Darkman; he whirled in time to see Hopewell, still clutching the girl, bend over and snatch up a shotgun. He raised it with one hand, John Wayne style, a leering grin of satisfaction creasing his face. "Death to the devil," he croaked, aiming the barrel at Darkman's heart.

Darkman squeezed his eyes shut as a shot roared. When he opened them again a millisecond later, Hopewell's forehead was exploding in a wet red spray, splashing the floor and wall. His legs came unhinged, and he fell over as Shawna scurried away from him on all fours.

Darkman snapped his head around. A tall man stood in the doorway between two bodies, a big pistol clutched in both hands, cop-style. He swung around slightly and aimed his weapon at Darkman.

"Hands in the air, Westlake," he growled. "Tell your people to drop their guns."

The old man and woman just off to Darkman's right dropped their shotguns. Their hands went up over their heads, and they dropped to the floor.

"The rest of you, do the same," the cop blared. "On the floor. Now!"

"You've got this all wrong," Darkman said evenly. This guy looked mad enough to do just about anything. "I'm not a member of this group."

"On the floor!"

Darkman was about to be humiliated when Julie burst past the cop and rushed over to Shawna. She swept her up, already in tears. "Thank God you're alive," she sobbed, hugging her tight in her strange garb of bedsheet and bruises.

The cop aimed his pistol at Darkman.

"No!" Julie cried. "Don't you see? He's not wearing a robe! The man in the red robe is the cult leader, and he's already dead!"

The cop deliberated for a moment, his eyes flicking back and forth. Martin Clayborne appeared suddenly and put a hand over the barrel of the cop's gun, forcing it down. His eyes, when he saw Darkman, registered instant shock.

Julie stepped toward Darkman while Shawna sobbed against her collarbone. "Peyton, are you okay?"

He turned his head, thankful that the spotlight was not casting its glow on what remained of his face. "Yes," he said. "Just . . . don't look at me."

"Oh, Peyton," she moaned. In her voice he heard the dwindling memory of the past—the good times they'd had, the nights they'd shared—and he knew with utter certainty that even with a permanent face and a man's real hands he could never bring back those days again.

The cop strode over, pulling a pair of handcuffs out of his pocket. He stepped behind Darkman and reached for his wrists.

"No!" Julie cried. "He saved Shawna! Don't you see?"

"Jesus," the cop growled. He took Darkman by the elbow and pulled him outside.

He went willingly enough, stumbling over bodies, not caring what happened to him now. The madness was over; he would not have to be Darkman anymore. He would simply be no one at all. He would be locked up in jail for the rest of his life for having murdered so many people who deserved to die.

"My name is Detective Sam Weatherspoon," the cop informed him when they were outside. Distantly, Darkman was aware of a siren. More cops were on their way—probably a lot more cops. "You are under arrest."

Suddenly Julie was there too. Martin was behind her, holding tightly to Shawna. They made a good-looking family, the three of them, Darkman observed silently. Maybe they would adopt Shawna and help her get over this tragedy by giving her a new home and a big dose of love.

"How can you arrest him?" Julie practically screamed.

Weatherspoon went for his wrists again. "Grand theft auto, to start with. And then there's the matter of a few murders. We'll see what . . ." His voice died away.

Darkman realized that the siren was coming closer,

coming fast. He looked toward the driveway and saw a big car coming straight at them, its headlights flashing as it bounced across the lawn, its tires spitting out greenish streamers of mud and mulch. What the hell?

He grabbed Julie and hurled her out of the way. Martin Clayborne leaped to one side, pulling Shawna to safety. Only Weatherspoon stood in defiance as the car shot close. But in the end his common sense prevailed, and he threw himself to one side.

Darkman rolled on the ground and sat up in time to see the car blast through the doorway of the guest cottage in an explosion of wood and plaster. Several people screamed. The car engine blatted as the driver reversed direction, pulling the snout of the car out of the wreckage.

Darla Dalton stuck her head out the window, her gorgeous black hair blowing across her face while inside the car fabulous colors danced and whirled.

"Is your ugly hide worth fifty grand?" she hollered at Darkman.

He shot to his feet. Maybe there was still time left to be Darkman after all, still time to do some good in a world so bad.

He launched himself through the open window of the Chrysler just as she ducked. His head rammed into the window on the opposite side, which was unfortunately closed. It shattered with a loud crunch, and pebbles of glass belched out onto the grass.

"Do it!" he shouted, squirming into a sitting position. "Go!"

She was already going. The Chrysler slewed into a wild U-turn, and she fought to straighten the wheel while crazy colors flashed across her face. The gearshift clunked, and she peeled out in a fresh spray of ruined grass.

Darkman heard a shot. A huge hole exploded through the rear window. Another. A hailstorm of glass attacked his missing face like a cloud of bees as he watched the cop aim again.

Weatherspoon fired but missed.

The car thumped over a curb and onto the asphalt. The tires screamed. Then Darla cut a hard right and they were barreling down the mountain road.

"Hey, Darla?" Darkman shouted against the roaring wind.

She looked at him. The expression on her face was one he had seen only once before—on the face of A. J. Foyt when he aced the Indy 500 in 1977.

"Yeah?"

He wished he had a face to smile with. "Think you could ever fall for a guy like me?"

She eyeballed him some more. "Can you really be anybody you want to be?"

He nodded.

"Robert Redford?" she said. "Tom Cruise?"

"Anybody you want."

"One of the Rockefellers?"

"Anybody."

"Well, then," she said as she rolled her window up, "I guess I could fall for you."

They took the back roads to the heart of the city and parked inside one of the loading docks of the abandoned soap factory Darkman called home.

EPILOGUE

The airport was nearly deserted on this cool, drizzly night, and Don Crawford, one of the many airport security officers who manned the metal detector at the entrance to the boarding areas, was nearly asleep on his feet. The hardest part of his job was this night shift business. Don liked wearing the uniform, liked having a gun on his belt, liked the feeling of power it gave him, but in his two years here he had never found anything more suspicious than a set of steak knives hidden in someone's luggage. He had almost given up hoping that a hijacker or a terrorist would try to pass through his electronic arch. It would be great to see his face in the paper—Don Crawford, heroic airport security officer.

At about 2:00 A.M. a tall man escorted a very beautiful woman toward Officer Crawford's station. Crawford shook himself awake and flicked the switch that turned the metal detector on. Instead of passing through it, though, the woman sidled up to him and smiled in his face. "Is this the right gate for the last red-eye to Rio tonight?" she crooned in his face.

He nodded, well aware of the schedule after two years

of standing here. Man, but did this babe smell good. Her slinky red dress was so tight it looked as if she'd been washed and tumble-dried in it. She had the blackest hair and the smoothest skin he had ever laid eyes on, and in the airport security business, he got to see a lot of babes.

Not anxious to make her traveling partner mad, Don made sure to be very professional. You could never know when a lawsuit might crop up from the ranks of these rich types.

Suddenly he almost swallowed his tongue. Christ almighty, her boyfriend was the frigging chief of police, standing right there beside her in the flesh. Don Crawford was no cop, but he'd been toying with the idea of applying to the academy to get out of this boring airport job. Chief Goodrow could grease those wheels, you bet.

"Sir," Don barked as he made his spine ramrod stiff. "A pleasure to see you here. Vacationing in Rio this year?"

"No, my daughter and I are working on a case. She's just in from Rio, but in the confusion she left her handbag at gate B-twenty-three, we think. Mind if we run down and check?"

"Not at all," Don said. "By all means."

They skirted the detector and strolled away. Don watched Chief Goodrow's daughter until she was out of sight. He wondered what it would be like to be the chief's son-in-law, but no, he was just plain old Don Crawford, and he could never hope for a woman with that much beauty and class.

A few minutes later they came back. "Did you find the handbag?" Don called out.

"Yes," the chief said. "But I think there might be some trouble. There's a chubby little guy down there waiting for a plane, and I think I spotted the shape of a gun in his pocket."

Don's face went pale. Had a gun slipped past him? Two years on the job, two years of waiting and hoping, and a gun had slipped past him? No. Please God, no.

"I'm on it, Chief," he barked, and sped away.

Chief Goodrow and Darla Dalton, neither of whom had any right to their names, walked to the main concourse and made their way outside. A big red Cadillac was parked at the curb in front of a row of idling taxicabs. The chief ignored the car and stopped at one of the cabs. He opened the back door.

"Care for a late-night martini?" he asked Darla.

"I believe that would hit the spot," she replied sweetly.

They got in. Even as the cab was leaving the airport it was passed by a short convoy of speeding police cars whose colorful lights were blipping and flashing against the darkness of the night.

"Seems to be trouble behind us," Darkman said casually to the cabbie, who nodded.

"Probably some freaking hijacker waving a gun around," he said. "Some damn fool wanting a free ride to Cuba. Let's just hope they nail him and nail him hard."

Chief Goodrow looked at Darla. She looked at him.

The cabbie looked back at them both. Considering how late it was and how gloomy the weather was, he could not understand why they looked so carefree.